△

THE YOUNG IN
THEIR COUNTRY

AND OTHER STORIES

To Irene,
With warm regards,

THE YOUNG IN THEIR COUNTRY
AND OTHER STORIES

RICHARD CUMYN

Rich

ENFIELD
&WIZENTY

Kingston,
Nov. 1, 2010

Copyright © 2010 Richard Cumyn

Enfield & Wizenty
(an imprint of Great Plains Publications)
345-955 Portage Avenue
Winnipeg, MB R3G 0P9
www.greatplains.mb.ca

Great Plains Publications gratefully acknowledges the financial support provided for its
publishing program by the Government of Canada through the Book Publishing Industry
Development Program (BPIDP); the Canada Council for the Arts; the Province of Manitoba
through the Book Publishing Tax Credit and the Book Publisher Marketing Assistance Program;
and the Manitoba Arts Council.

Design & Typography by Relish Design Studio Ltd.

Printed in Canada by Friesens

Front cover image © Anna Cumyn, photographer

FIRST EDITION

Library and Archives Canada Cataloguing in Publication

Cumyn, Richard, 1957-
    The young in their country : and other stories / Richard Cumyn.

Short stories.
ISBN 978-1-926531-02-1

    I. Title.

PS8555.U4894Y69 2010   C813'.54   C2010-903230-6

Mixed Sources
Cert no. SW-COC-001271
© 1996 FSC
FSC

ENVIRONMENTAL BENEFITS STATEMENT

Great Plains Publications saved the following
resources by printing the pages of this book on
chlorine free paper made with 100% post-consumer
waste.

TREES	WATER	SOLID WASTE	GREENHOUSE GASES
8	3,566	217	740
FULLY GROWN	GALLONS	POUNDS	POUNDS

Calculations based on research by Environmental Defense and the Paper Task Force.
Manufactured at Friesens Corporation

FOR SHARON

CONTENTS

◭

FAMILY DAY

FAMILY DAY

▲

EVEN IN THE dark and across the field separating the house from the road, I knew it was her car. The death rattle of the engine gave it away. I could make out the molded plastic ski-case strapped to the roof and the distinctive slope to the vehicle's rear end. She adored that old Swedish bolt-bucket the way you clutch the memory of an old flame. Someone at the Department of Motor Vehicles was going to have to condemn it before she'd ever give it up. Howard, my hired man, usually slipped the car a litre of oil when he thought she wasn't looking.

I went outside to pull Zeno, our Weimaraner, off the hood of the Saab, so that Coralene could bring the car ahead and park in a space between the house and the stable. When she got out, she let the dog drape his paws over her shoulders and lick her face before I sent him away to chase a stick. We dubbed his colouring Sunburned Mole.

She looked, as she always did when she came to the farm, like gentry: knee-high leather riding boots, oxblood red; tight black jeans; oatmeal coloured tweed jacket hanging a little loose, with brown-leather patches at the elbows and over the right shoulder. Her hair was a lustrous silver-blond held back in a severe ponytail. Her only makeup was bright red lipstick, a beacon in the washed-out February landscape.

"Say something intelligent," she said. "I'm about to lose it."

"'The quality of mercy is not strained. It droppeth as the gentle rain from heaven upon the place beneath.'"

"I'm telling you, Keith, four hours trapped listening to idiots, blowhards and yappers, not to mention my own ranting voice. How are you?"

We embraced. "Fine," I said. "Didn't you bring music to listen to?"

"It's all packed away. I couldn't even find Howard's pal on the dial, the one who sings the farm report."

We walked back to get her things out of the trunk. She had a large burgundy-coloured suitcase upholstered in rip-proof fabric, a heavy wicker food-hamper, a pair of dark-green Wellingtons and her small single-barrel Remington. She picked up the gun in its black, zippered case. I frowned at the sight of it and at her "Don't give me that look" look. We had argued about the weapon before, to an uneasy stalemate. If she really needed to kill something, why didn't she go after a defenseless paper target at an indoor firing range? But to press her on the matter might have kept her away, and our time together was dwindling before she left for the bottom of the world.

"I should warn you," I said. "If Hilda has her way, you're never leaving."

She stood the shotgun in the corner of the kitchen beside the back door and went to hug Natasha, Howard's wife, who turned from where she was standing at the sink. Natasha held her yellow-gloved hands out to the side in an awkward gesture of one pinned in place by love. She had Coralene's slim build and was the same height, a younger version by forty years.

Howard bellowed hello from outside the open door. He was reminding me more and more, in appearance and temperament, of the American humourist, Roy Blount, Jr. Howard rarely entered the farmhouse, he and Natasha having their own winterized cabin on the property, where they ate and slept. As caretakers they had the farm to themselves most of the week. Since her arrival two summers before, I'd been trying to get Natasha reading to improve her English, but she insisted that the "Tee-Fee" was a more effective educational tool than any old book.

"I had it serviced last week, Howard," said Coralene, in a tone that said she knew he was going to get his head and shoulders in under the hood of her car anyway.

"Am so happy to see you, Cora. Sorry to have, like, such wet hands." Natasha's low throaty giggle did little to dispel her permanent pout. She looked and acted more like Howard's daughter than his wife; given the difference in their ages, such a relationship was entirely plausible.

"Hilda's put you upstairs," I said. I was standing just inside the entrance, Coralene's suitcase standing upright beside me, her basket in one hand and her rubber boots in the other. Natasha leapt on the hamper and began to unpack its contents. As she pulled out a loaf of black rye bread and a large Polish sausage, she gave a squeal of delight.

"We have another guest this weekend. One of my clients."

"It's fine. I didn't give you much warning. I'll sleep wherever you put me, Keith. I'll even snuggle under the covers with Natasha if that's what's called for. Howard would like that, wouldn't he." She smiled impishly.

"Not my scene no more," said Natasha, chin-down, the under-whites of her eyes cloudy and disapproving. Coralene wrapped her again in a disarming hug.

The house, mid-nineteenth century, could sleep eight comfortably in four large bedrooms, and for such guests as Coralene who were not in my care there was a sleeping cabin far enough away to afford them some privacy. It was hidden in a cedar grove, with little evidence it existed aside from a barely noticeable footpath leading to it. Spring and summer, as long as it was vacant, it was my retreat, the place where I read papers, wrote reports and napped in the afternoon. Before we knew Coralene was coming for the long weekend—the Monday was the newly designated provincial holiday, "Family Day"—we'd decided to put Patsy (not her real name), a twenty-year-old mother of three, in the guest cabin. She'd requested an isolated room while her maxillofacial bruising healed. She had driven up from Kingston with Hilda and me the day before, a Friday afternoon, and Natasha helped her settle in. Howard, a former Joyceville guard I'd met while doing some work in the prison, knew to hang back until my clients felt comfortable enough to approach him. Few of them did.

Patsy came into the kitchen a few minutes after Natasha took our guest upstairs. Without acknowledging me she approached the refrigerator. Stopping, not reaching to open it, she paused like someone many times her age who had forgotten the reason why she'd come into the room. She was about to say something when Hilda and Coralene entered, hand-in-hand, each in delighted possession of the other, with

Natasha following. Natasha finished washing and drying the dinner dishes. Patsy picked a Clementine orange out of the fruit bowl on the counter, looked at it, put it back, glanced at me as she passed, and went outside.

"Did we interrupt something?" said Hilda.

"I'm not sure," I said. "I think she needs to talk."

"Spectacular colouring," said Coralene, who despite her jocular tone was shaken by the sight of the girl's contusions. Natasha put the dish rack away and slipped quietly out of the room.

Hilda said, "Don't let us keep you, Keith, if you need to have a session," as she fixed Coralene a plate of leftovers.

"It doesn't appear to be urgent," I said, "and I can't leave without toasting the prodigal sister."

"We'll never see her again. Her timing could not possibly be worse. It's clear to me she is doing this on purpose. She knows I'm retiring next month. We were supposed to spend our golden years together." Hilda said this while looking directly at her sister. She turned a look of mock exasperation on me. "You don't expect me to pass every waking minute with him, do you?"

I poured us each a generous glassful of red wine and we drank to Coralene's adventure. A hospital in Christchurch wanted her badly enough to pay her a full-year's, administrator's salary for eight months' residence. She was going to spend the rest of the time crewing on her many friends' yachts all over the watery world.

"You mustn't be gloomy," she admonished her sister. "You always were an old gloom-puss. Think about it: this will be your excuse to travel. The flight is virtually nonstop. Meanwhile, you'll have all this time to enjoy your horses, read what you want, sleep late. And despite what you say, I know how much you've been looking forward to spending time with your brilliant husband."

"Don't make me laugh," said Hilda.

I thanked Coralene with a smile and a raised glass, taking the compliment for what it was, as much mollification as tribute.

"We're going to miss you terribly, that's all," said Hilda. "What about Mick? I thought you two bought a house together."

"Mack. He's buying me out. It was never meant to be permanent, Hilda, not that I have anything against permanence. In others."

"You're running from something, clearly," I said, topping them up.

"Stop being the psychologist, will you, and tell her she has to stay. Sick Kids is the best in the world at what they do, you said so yourself, Cor. You've saved its neck countless times. How can you go? I mean, come on, you love Toronto. It's finally filled its own shoes. You can't tell me your work there is done, that there are no challenges left."

"My work there is done. There are no challenges left."

"Do something, you unhelpful man. Convince her."

"Oceans to cross," I offered.

"He's not even going to make an effort," said Hilda. She sipped from her glass and moved close enough to slip an arm through her sister's. "Oh, poop. We're glad you're here. We will hold on to this time and not think about what's to come."

"Sis never did like to plan," said Coralene. "It was terrible to watch you sometimes, seeing you paralyzed by what was coming at you. You would block your ears and hum and focus instead on something nearby and intensely small."

"She thinks I'm still five and wetting my pants."

"You never told me about that," I said. "This changes everything."

"I was speaking figuratively."

"Sounded pretty literal to me."

"Don't you have somewhere to go? Behaviour to modify, reports to write?"

"I know when I'm not wanted," I said, playing up the pout.

"Don't be taken in, Cor. He's a master manipulator."

"Stay, Keith, she doesn't mean it," said our visitor, although she didn't try very hard to dissuade me from leaving.

I kissed them in turn, letting them know without saying so that I knew how much they needed to be alone and that I would if not happily then contentedly find something to do. I would see what Patsy needed. I'd recently installed an electric heater, a faux potbelly stove, in the cabin where she was staying, and was curious to see how well it worked. I lifted my coat off its hook near the back door, donned the garment, tested a large 6-volt flashlight, and went outside.

The day's brief thaw having reverted, my footsteps crunched through a frangible muddy crust. Zeno came out of his doghouse to the limit of his tether, whining to be included in the escapade. I untied him, but held him by his leather collar. "Stay close. No gallivanting." When I released my grip, the hound took off down the driveway after something only he could sense. He ignored my calls; it was time to get tough with him, I decided, for his own safety. Obedience class, first thing tomorrow.

I heard footsteps coming from the right and shone my light at the sound. Patsy put a hand in front of her face and I lowered the beam to a spot on the ground in front of her.

"I miss my brats," she blurted without preamble. No establishing sigh, not even the ubiquitous "so" that led verbal communication those days. "He's coming to pick me up."

"That wasn't the deal. You were going to stay the weekend, to give the process a chance."

"I know. I know I agreed and everything. It's … I'm not ready to be on my own yet. I can't be here."

"They won't let you see your children, you know that. Not until after you've healed. And I'm not talking about your face, Patsy. They're safe where they are now. If you lead him to them…"

Zeno had returned via a tortuous route through the front fields and a windbreak of weed trees and scrub brush. He looked up at me and let out a yowl: What's the hold-up? Why are we standing still?

"I'm really sorry. I know I screwed up. Again. But he feels so bad about everything. He loves me, he said so, and I love him. I can help him be better. He just needs me not to be so clingy and stuff and to not smother him. He has so many worries, he doesn't need me nagging in his ear all the time."

"You're not ready and neither is he. Call him. Tell him to turn around and go home, at least for tonight. We'll see where we're sitting tomorrow."

"You have your guest to entertain."

"She entertains herself. Don't go looking elsewhere for justification. You have to take control of your situation. How long ago did he call?" I tried to estimate the driving time from where they lived, a few kilometers outside of Gananoque.

"I called him."

"And you gave him directions."

"You said yourself I'm not a prisoner here. If at any point I felt I couldn't go through with…."

"You agreed that if you couldn't stay here I'd take you to a shelter in the city."

"I don't need a fucking shelter, I need to see my kids. I need to make shit right with my man."

"You can't do that until you make things right with yourself."

I called for Zeno, waited, called again. I couldn't see or hear him. "Let's at least get out of the cold," I said, and began walking in the direction of her cabin. "Coming?" She hesitated. She didn't want me in the little room with her when her husband arrived. I wasn't going to concede the point; her call to him had the potential to reverse all the progress we'd made back in the city. She was close to a breakthrough but still delicate. I couldn't have her sprout wings only to fly back into the candle flame.

Behind us came the sound of a car starting up and a car door closing. Zeno barked from somewhere in the vicinity of the car: Howard and Natasha often took him with them when they went into Kingston, where a certain pet store lavished homemade treats on the hound.

"Hold on," I said to Patsy. "Go in and get warm. Leave the light off. Will you do that for me, please? Make yourself some tea. Put on some music." She gave a shrug of ambiguous meaning. "I have to ask Howard something. I'll be back in a minute. You and I aren't finished talking."

"Oh, I'm pretty sure we are."

Natasha was outside the vehicle and giving Zeno the attention both of them knew he deserved. In another quarter minute I was close enough to be heard.

"So sorry, doctor, he can't come with, not this time. Not let him—no, they won't, will they, darling, yes, beautiful Zinno—into movie house. Is okay?"

When Howard opened his door and stood up, the dog jumped into the car.

"How long will you be gone?"

"Couple hours," he said. "Three at the most. We figured, what with you and the missus here and your sister-in-law, we could make ourselves scarce for a bit. I cleared it with Hilda. It's not going to be a problem, is it? We could go another night." Natasha stood, crossed her arms and turned away from us.

"No, you're right, we are perfectly capable of holding the fort here for a few hours." I reached into the back seat and hauled Zeno out by his collar. For all the manhandling he was receiving, he continued to love everyone he touched. "Go on," I ordered, "run it off, you nut." He obeyed, sprinting back down the track towards the guest cabin, veering into the bushes, making crashing sounds like that of glass breaking as he knocked branches together and sent their ice skins shattering on the brittle ground.

"You sure?"

I told them they should stick to their plan, have themselves a wonderful evening, and in the morning provide me with a detailed critical account of the film. We'd be fine without them.

Zeno chased them down the driveway to the road. I held my breath as Howard stopped, signaled a left turn, and slowly pulled out, no doubt watching to see what the dog was going to do. Zeno, to his credit, let his quarry escape. His sprint up the long approach to the house was soundless in the bright cold moonlight that had breached the cloud cover. As he got closer I heard him, a bellows, his claws grabbing the frozen ground and flicking bits of gravel and ice behind him. With each stride his long lean body folded and opened like the movement of an elegant machine. He ran straight at me for no other reason but to cover the distance in the shortest possible time, brag about it with his slobbery tongue and be congratulated for being alive.

He ran headlong towards me, close enough to risk being touched or caught, but veered out of reach at the last second. I lunged at him— I knew to really try lest the dog be disappointed in my half-hearted effort—and missed. I wanted to get him tied again to the long line attached to his doghouse, and so put all the urgent authority I could muster into my voice when I called him. He knew the game was up. His brief attempt to prolong it was a weak one and, tired out, he returned willingly, seeking out my hands, allowing me to pat him, smooth down his back and flanks, rub behind his ears. After such a hearty run he would tuck himself into the nest of old blankets I'd made for him in his house and sleep, the temperatures at night having risen enough that he could stay out there safely and thrive in the fresh air. I could almost believe he was thinking about sleep now, as I crouched beside him, kneading the supple muscles in his neck and shoulders and assuming in error that I didn't have to hold him by the collar.

He heard the car approaching before I turned my head and saw the light, and in that instant he was gone. I shouted at him to heel, amazed that he still had the energy to bolt at top speed towards the vehicle. I ran after him, quickening my pace, but he wouldn't be caught. The car moved as quickly as it would have been travelling on the road, the rural route that led north from Kingston, far too fast for the farm's driveway with its many ruts and dips. Zeno was a grey ghost in the headlights. I didn't recognize the vehicle, but had a good idea whose it was.

Zeno's shrill yelp made me start. I'd lost sight of him for a second and now I had to step back, partway into the drainage ditch, to avoid being hit as the car sped past, its chassis bouncing crazily. The driver could not have missed seeing me walking towards him, the strong beam of light fanning outwards from my hand. I'd been careful to keep the light trained on the road ahead and not shine it in the driver's eyes. Whoever it was, he hadn't extended me the same courtesy.

I caught a glimpse of him in profile, though my eyes were still adjusting to the lower light; when I closed them I saw twin fireballs. He had closely cropped hair, possibly shaved or bald, a prominent jaw, and a spotty bloom of facial hair. He didn't turn to look in my direction as he passed.

I climbed out of the snow-filled ditch and heard Zeno's whimper. It took a few sweeps with the light to find him. He was lying on his side in the ditch on the other side of the road and was struggling to stand. He yipped and whined as I approached and I wondered what he was trying to tell me. Maybe it was that I should approach with caution, that he couldn't say what deep instinct might take hold of him, what those jaws might do. It was going to be awkward getting him out of the ditch without hurting him or both of us. I shone the light over the area: no blood at least. He was shivering, in shock but eager to do what the alpha male required of him. Hilda and her sister would have laughed to hear me voice such a notion; I was about as alpha as a child's wooden letter-block.

His whining had the urgency of a plea. As I stepped into the depression, my boots slid towards him and he pushed himself up with trembling hindquarters. I fell backwards, startling him and making him recoil farther down the ditch and away from the house. He struggled in the deep wet snow, trying to muster the power that would propel him over the top. Finally, after two failed attempts, he scrambled out onto the drive. I climbed out, too, having retrieved my lamp, which I shone in his direction.

"Where are you going?" I called, as if he were an inebriated colleague searching for his parked car. "This way. Zeno! Here boy! Zeno, Zeno come!"

He stopped and turned haltingly, showing me what I'd been unable to see before, that his stance was now three-legged. I felt nauseated with rage.

"Hold tight, boy, I'm going to bring you back." I could have said anything; the tone carried the meaning. Soft, low voice, oblique approach, never head-on. I couldn't risk giving him the impression that I was attacking. He didn't understand why he felt so bad, why he couldn't put pressure on his paw. For the first time I felt certain I could take a life. The anger swelled and crashed over me, a short-lived, violent breaker.

Zeno let me get only so close before tottering away. He tried the damaged leg and quickly drew it back up. I was surprised at how little sound he made. We repeated the dance steps of approach and retreat until I stopped and waited, thinking, *Let him come to me*, but he wouldn't let himself be caught. I walked slowly back towards the house, leading him in that direction, a span of twenty meters or so between us. If I walked too quickly the animal lost heart, sitting and signalling his distress with a bark. I imagined him indicting me for my part in the nasty enterprise that encompassed anger, jealousy, hurtling steel, incomprehensible pain and a foreleg that no longer did what it was supposed to. But I wanted to believe that he was saying also that he trusted me to make it better once we were bathed again in light and warmth.

He refused to come in the house, preferring to hover just outside the cone of light spilling from the back door, which I had found ajar. I locked it behind me and called hello, as Howard had done earlier, sending my voice into the empty kitchen and out into the rooms beyond. "We're in here." Hilda's strained voice. "In here" meant the parlour, a small room not large or conveniently enough located to be a dining room, and too dark to be a place for socializing. We'd put a small TV and music player in the room, with three armchairs. I found Hilda and Coralene seated there, their faces tense though by their postures they might have been described as lounging.

"Where is he? Did he come in? The creep hit Zeno. I'm calling the O.P.P. and the vet, in that order."

"Please don't do that," said Hilda. I could tell that her sister wanted to be the one to relay that caution, that this transcended the usual modifying comment a wife might address to her husband about his behaviour. "Why weren't you here?" Hilda continued. "What could you have been doing all this time?"

"Trying to coax the dog home. I think he has a broken leg. Where is he now?"

"Who, the dog?" Hilda was trembling, her eyes wide and fixed on me, as if she couldn't believe I'd committed a monumentally stupid act.

"You didn't tell him where she is," I said.

"Have I ever told you how much I hate it that you bring these ... ugly broken people into our home?"

"It's not our home, Hilda, it's a treatment facility I use in my work."

"This is my home, this is where I grew up. I don't care what status you've given it for tax or legal purposes. Why can't you..."

"I am. I will, the day I retire. We've been over this. The property reverts to us." Three years before, to finance my program and draw a strict ethical line, Hilda had let me sell the farm to the province, with the proviso that we could buy it back for a nominal fee once the facility was no longer operating. The proceeds of the "sale," essentially a government grant, paid for Howard and Natasha's room-and-board and their paltry salaries and covered the insurance and property tax. We were allowed to sublet some of the fields to a neighbour as pasture for his dairy cows. As a private psychotherapist I didn't bill the health system. I charged my clients— men and women, whom I treated separately and sometimes as couples—a small fee. We lived comfortably on Hilda's salary and would continue to do so on our pensions. I was at most two years away from closing up shop. She had only to hang on that long.

"What did he do?"

"Nothing," she said, glancing at Coralene and then—it stood out in both their expressions—regretting it immediately.

"He told us that if we left this room or called the police we'd regret it. His exact words were, 'You'll be sorry,'" said Coralene, who let a snigger escape through her nose. It was uncontrollable, the sort of laughter that overwhelms children in situations of high tension or solemnity. "Forgive me, it's just that I haven't heard that expression since we were kids. 'You'll ... be ... sorr-ree!'"

"Tell him what he did to you."

"I'm fine, Hilda."

"She has deep bruises. On both arms. And he took her gun. He made her give him the bullets." Hilda was beginning to hyperventilate.

"Shells, Hilda. Shotgun *shells*."

"Okay," I said. "It's going to be—you told him where she is. He might not find the path in the dark. But she called him to come get her, so it might be all right. God, I wish you'd left that thing at home."

"It was going to be my last time firing it, Keith. I can't take it with me. I was leaving it with you, to do with it what you will. You've had coyotes on the property—I thought perhaps Howard could take charge of it. He is trained to use one, after all. It was going to be up to you. If you wanted to, you could have turned it in to the police or, you know, into a ploughshare."

"We can't risk spooking him," I said. "As soon as we hear them drive away we call the local detachment."

"What if they don't drive away?" said Coralene. "What if only he drives away? After he shoots her?"

"He's not going to do that."

"How do you know? How can you be so sure?"

They stood. My arrival had both freed them from the intruder's injunction and heightened their anxiety. They took turns going over to the small window, which gave them no glimpse of what the angry young man might be doing. It was better than sitting motionless. They hugged each other and themselves, as much for warmth as reassurance. The old house had its cold rooms and this was one, despite the dry, quartered splits of hardwood that burned brightly in the small fireplace. Natasha saw to that sort of thing; given her way, she would have a fire burning in every room, available hearth or no. In this sunless salon you had to be standing directly in front of the grate to feel the slightest warmth.

"You can't let him do anything to her, Keith." This came from Coralene. Hilda, I assumed, would be glad to see the last of Patsy, her goon of a husband, and every other perpetrator, victim and troubled parent who might require refuge in my landlocked ark. She tolerated what I did. That sounds uncharitable. She was always a kind hostess, a sympathetic presence. She'd promised to take Patsy riding if the girl felt up to it. Those who came here to get better often opened up to Hilda in ways they didn't with me. But she was saying she'd had enough. She wanted her life in retirement to be different. She wanted her farm back, for our use alone. She wanted to raise her horses, teach riding, and have me present when she desired my company. Who could blame her? I'd been available to all except her, at a phone call's notice, at any time of day or week. I had the feeling that if she could she'd install a steel gate across the farm's entrance after these two troubled souls had gone, padlock it and never open it to a stranger again.

I told them what Patsy had said to me outside. I knew she wasn't ready to live with the man again, if ever, but she blamed herself for her injuries and believed fiercely that only she could change him. She would need more than a heavy curtain drawn across the recent past, obliterating memory. How many times had I heard a woman claim that it was all her fault or that it was the result of something external to the family, an evil having infiltrated the man to turn him into someone she no longer recognized? Turn back the clock, she prayed, as if the clock, the maddening one that grew louder with every tick, hadn't begun the instant he first raised his fist against her.

Hilda looked at me as if to say that this was my fault and I should fix it, pronto. That she knew Zeno was outside, hurt and needing attention, and didn't immediately rush out to comfort the dog, told me how traumatized she'd been made to feel by the man.

Coralene was hunched over trying to see out the inadequate window. "If she called him, why did he take my shotgun? I don't get it," she said. "We didn't try to keep her from him. What's he playing at?"

We stayed too long in that oppressive little room. The fire reduced to coals. Hilda huddled under an old afghan, her feet tucked under her. Coralene stood with her right hand on her left shoulder, left hand cupping the opposite elbow. She might have been a field marshal visualizing a troop assault, the way she would bring her right fist to her mouth, squint, and furrow her brow. She repeated, "What's his game? What's the bugger up to? We should have heard them drive away by now."

I went out to the front entrance to listen. That door, rarely used, was always locked. Two tall narrow sidelights framed it. Hilda had placed two spiky ferns in large pots to either side and they'd grown tall enough in the west-facing exposure to obscure a good part of each window. I liked the style enough to reproduce it in my guest-cabin office. My glass blocks created a less welcoming, more defensive effect. I'd wanted to bring in the light but also establish a barrier, something that would make the occupant feel protected.

Night had turned the window glass to mirrors as I approached, a rumpled, blurry figure dressed in wool sweater, worn jeans and foliage. Outside, a brief flagstone-path led to the door, allowing a quiet approach, no wooden steps or reverberating plank porch signaling arrival. And so, even though I was acting like a security guard checking the various points of his assigned round, I was startled to hear the door knocker strike its brass plate.

I opened it without thinking: proof of sixty-seven years of living to an ingrained code of politeness and hospitality. A knock comes at the door, it must be answered. It took me to the count of five before I recognized Natasha standing there. It wasn't that she had changed appearance. She was simply the last person I expected to see there.

It's Howard, she said. Howard is dead. What? I said. Are you sure? Tell me what happened. The story came out scrambled at first, how she had found our kitchen door locked, how in a panic she had left her key in her purse. Where was the purse? Back in the car, she said. Howard had yelled at her and the car had got stuck. The woman drove her home and why didn't Howard believe she could do it? Do what? Model, she said. All right, I said, slow down. From the beginning.

The fight had begun before they'd gotten into the car. Natasha had said, innocently enough, that she'd like to try her hand modeling clothes. You don't know the first thing about how to be a model, Howard said. Are you saying I'm not pretty enough? No, he said, that's not it. He had not released her from the vicious pimps who had brought her to this country only to have her drift back into that that work, that wretched life. It wasn't work, he yelled. Slavery! They didn't pay her except in drugs to keep her from straying.

Howard and Natasha didn't make it very far before she demanded he stop the car to let her out. Where was she going? I'm walking home, she said. Stop the car. I'll stop when you promise never to go back to that life. It's not that life, she said, it's legitimate. It's the world of fashion. You don't hear anything I say.

He stopped the car by the side of the road, parked, and let the engine idle. I do think you're beautiful, he said. I'm sorry. I don't want men looking at you. Not men, women, she said. I want to wear pretty things and get away from this place from time to time. That's all. Not forever and for all time. There isn't enough for me to do here, she said, and besides, being around those women, his patients, it gives me a bad feeling. It brings back too many bad memories.

They talked for a few minutes more, Natasha reassuring Howard that she would always be there with him, that the last thing she wanted was to live without him, her saviour. Howard began to relax. They agreed to continue to Kingston. They still had time to catch the showing of the movie they'd wanted to see. But when he accelerated, signaling to get back on the road, he found that his right-hand wheels were stuck in the loose gravel and semi-frozen sand of the shoulder, which dropped off in a steep slope to a drainage ditch.

Howard grew angry again, blaming the predicament on Natasha. She took his place at the steering wheel while he tried to push the car from the back right corner. The front right wheel had sunk such that the car's body was touching the dirt. He moved forward, lifting and pushing, telling her to straighten her front wheels and press slowly on the accelerator. The car surged and rocked that way, only to tear up more of the shoulder and sink deeper. Howard had been grunting, swearing, calling encouragement, stepping around to her side to guide her through the open window. Now she heard only the sound of the front wheels spinning with a gritty moan. She made two more surges before stopping. She listened. Howard? What do we do now, Howard?

He was kneeling when she found him, his right hand resting on the trunk of the car. It hurt, he gasped, all down his left arm and through his back. She tried but failed to lift him to his feet. She crouched beside him and they waited that way. What do I do, Howard? Tell me. His gritted teeth, his clenched body, as if to relax were to risk slipping into a torrent.

The heart attack stopped after a while. It seemed unending but might have been only a minute. She got him to stand, shuffle onto the road, get into the car and lie down on the back seat. She left the car running with the heater on and ran down the road to the nearest house. The woman who lived there drove Natasha back to Howard. "That man is dead," said the woman, as if she were explaining to a child why a TV doctor was pulling a sheet over a person's face. Natasha screamed at the poor woman, went at her with fists and nails. The woman held her wrists tightly until the fit passed and then she drove Natasha home, after shutting off the engine and locking the doors of Howard's car. She let Natasha off at the end of our lane.

"She didn't stay with you? She couldn't drive you up to the house?" said Coralene, who had emerged with Hilda at the first sound of Natasha's voice. "What about reporting this?"

"She said is better if maybe I tell police. Or you do it, please, doctor. I cannot think."

"Are you sure about Howard?" said Hilda.

"He did not breathe." She cried again, a series of hard, wrenching jags, the ferns swaying with her sobs. She stamped her foot on the scuffed hardwood, made wild movements with her head, swallowed her screams. She would not take any of our offers of comfort. She would not be led to a chair or relinquish her coat, hat or gloves. "How can I be here when he is still out there?" She didn't know the name of the woman who had driven her home. She wasn't even sure exactly where the car and Howard were.

"You mean she's going to drive past him on her way home and not do anything more?" said Coralene.

"I don't know," said Natasha in a hoarse whisper, "she don't tell me what she will do. She just wishes me all the luck in the world. That's the words she uses."

Hilda and her sister continued to stand near Natasha, helpless to diminish her grief. "Call now," they said. Natasha's arrival had jolted them out of their fearful state. Call. Bring in the organized world, bring uniformed officers who know what to do.

I was returning the receiver of the kitchen wall-phone to its cradle when I heard the sound of car tires on gravel and saw the illumination of headlights beyond the window above the sink. I went outside. I didn't know what I was going to do. The car stopped near Zeno's house, where the farm's long driveway turned and widened on its way down to the county road. I was thirty or forty paces away, behind them and closer to the house. The driver's door opened and as the youth emerged, the barrel of Coralene's Remington seemed to elongate in his right hand. It looked like an extension of his arm. The car idled, its lights washing the stable wall and nearby paddock.

I yelled, "Hey you!" and he turned. Because I was coming at him out of the dark, he probably couldn't see much more than the contrast of my form against the vaguer gloom behind me. "I want a word with you."

"No more words," he said, and fired into the dirt between us, sending shot and gravel flying against my boots and ankles. It felt as if I'd been cut with a switch. He fired again from waist level. I saw the ejected shell fly out sideways and felt a concussion of air followed by a sudden sharp burning sensation in my right thigh.

He was about to fire again when Zeno came out of his house and snarled. The shooter made a lurching quarter-turn towards the dog. Zeno's hair stood up in a roughened ridge along his neck and back. He touched his injured foreleg to the ground and immediately pulled it up. Patsy's door opened. Her husband yelled, "Close it!" She did. He returned his attention to the dog. As he was raising the barrel above his waist, Zeno, incredibly, lunged at him. The weapon went off. Zeno yelped and fell over like a heavy, tossed sack.

He turned the gun on me and said, "This is your fault. You did this, not me. Everything was fine until she came here. Remember that." I closed my eyes. He fired again, missing well wide. He got back in the car and drove, faster than he'd done on arrival. The brake lights flashed on and the vehicle skidded, fishtailing to a stop before reaching the road. The engine died and all light was extinguished. I stood bolted in place, hardly breathing, balance tentative. I couldn't bring myself to look at Zeno, who made no sound, or my wound, which felt liquid, warm and increasingly numb. The car was a blacker shape in the enveloping darkness. Everything was still. Someone arriving might have called it serene. A car, its engine ticking over, cooling, motionless at the edge of the property. A man, trying to stay upright on higher ground near the house, deafened by the drumming of his heart, sickened by the feeling of the dark stain saturating the fabric of his jeans. A dark heap, chocolate-on-silver, lying close by him in front of a miniature, peaked-roof house. No passing traffic, nothing in the sky, the lurking coyotes mute, the caretakers of the forest fast asleep.

A muffled explosion came from inside the car. Nothing happened for half a minute. Then it was as if someone had pushed a button that set the planet in motion again. The passenger-side door flew open and Patsy, moaning, stumbled out, fell, slid into the ditch, crawled up the other side and began running across the field, away from the car but not towards the house. Unable to stand any longer, I went into a crouch and toppled onto my left side. Their sirens preceded four police cruisers and an ambulance, all arriving from the south. The front door of the house opened. The women came out, got me to my feet and helped me inside, Hilda and Coralene taking my arms and weight across their shoulders and Natasha holding the bleeding limb off the ground. I kept trying to look back at the car, thinking the driver-side door was going to open. I wanted it to open. I wanted him to come running up the driveway, yelling like a crazed commando, firing his insupportable weapon until all his ammunition was spent. I thought, Let him stand before us and look about him and explain himself. An idiotic fantasy, it was like something out of *Tom Brown's School Days* or Horatio Alger. Account for yourself. Stand up and face your accusers. Be a man. Live the rest of your life in atonement. Stand up straight. Acknowledge the havoc you've unleashed.

That car door remained closed. Howard never again put oil in Coralene's Saab. Coralene gave the car to her ex, flew to New Zealand and has yet to return. Natasha worked as a chambermaid in a hotel in Toronto before marrying a man who owned an upholstery store on Dundas Street West. The police asked us the same questions many times in different ways. I buried the dog deep in the woods, where he was happiest, where the smells were most rewarding and the promise best of small, fast-moving quarry. We have an appointment next week with the Weimaraner breeder who sold us Zeno. We think we'll get a bitch pup this time. Patsy served two years of a five-year sentence for manslaughter. Her lawyer argued unsuccessfully that she had assisted in her husband's suicide, the state of the victim's oral and cranial cavities appearing to support that thesis. She and her children live with her parents now in the town of Sydenham. The surgeon who operated on me was able to remove most of the buck-shot from my thigh, and I'm being monitored for lead poisoning. I have a new hip, unrelated to the shooting. A colleague is helping me work through the fallout from the event, the recurring nightmares, my inability to focus and the fatigue that fells me like a cattle bolt at unexpected moments in the day.

I go into the maximum security prisons now, Kingston Penitentiary and Millhaven Institution, two or three times a month. On a good day a man will meet my gaze and hold it. On a really successful day our hour-long session will exhaust him like a series of wind sprints across an open field or a steady trudge up a high mountainside. If he breaks down crying, repentant or haunted by the tormentors of his past, I think, Good, cry. Let the stunned world hear your sobs. Beg its pity. Pray there's forgiveness left for the likes of you. If you are lucky, you will meet someone strong enough to pull the trigger for you, as you go down on your merciless redeemer.

OIL & SAND

OIL & SAND

Δ

SHE REMINDS ME of the way I used to be when I was on fire, when I could drink and work all night. She's built herself a big lean-to on the other side of the clearing near the spot where the four boys have pitched their tents and she's told me to stay away. She's working on something big, she says, something that will take her a long time, all summer, and if I sneak over there to look I'll wreck the wave.

She drives to town with Wiry Boy once a week or so, usually on rainy days when they aren't working, and she comes back with groceries and propane and the like. I look at her and she says, "What?" I don't want to know. She could be, but I doubt it. She's too caught up in her painting to think about anything else. And these four are here to earn the most money they can in the shortest time. Then it's back east to school. The one who stays all summer gets the William R. Cullen Prize for thickest skull. I'm pretty sure who it's going to be: the soft one who looks like that sappy folk singer: baby face and pouty lips under a black beard. Each of the other three, in his own way, is wound a few turns too tight to last.

Beard Baby looks deep like a quiet black pool in the forest. Something is going on inside that one. He's told himself that life is all about endurance. He's placed his own reward at the end of it all: if he sticks it out until first frost, he'll buy that sound system he's been dreaming about. He's not the one who owns the car. That's Wiry, the one who looks like he's been here before. I think he camped here a few days last summer, before moving into the trailers closer to town. The trailer camp has electricity and hot water. Showers. When I get too ripe Sylvie hauls me to the municipal pool and threatens to come into the men's change room to make sure I use soap and scrub all the hard-to-reach areas. She used to say that kind of thing with a glint in her eye.

She's started to ration my booze. Maybe I can get one of the college boys to slip me an extra *bouteille*. The third one, always has his beak in a Signet Shakespeare, he came over to borrow some rope after a heavy rainfall in early May. They'd bought a big tarp to hang over the two tents. We don't get all that much rain up here, but it all comes in a couple or three downpours. I told him to dig a ditch, a ravine, around their camp. He asked me where we got the picture window and I was too out of it to remember. He looked at me like he knew who I was but was too polite to ask. Hey, aren't you Bill Cullen, that famous painter nobody's ever heard of? We're all too polite. We never say what we mean or what we're really thinking. I asked him what he was reading and he said *Coriolanus* or some such, maybe *Titus Andronicus*, and took glee in describing the mayhem and gore that fills the play. "Do you ever go to see these beautiful old plays you're always reading?" I asked him, because I swear the other day it was *The Tempest* and the couple of days before that it was *Measure for Measure*. No, he said, he preferred reading and discussing them. He was studying for his master's in English, what else, and was almost positive he was going to be a professor. "Either that or a massage therapist." He smiled, big joke. He had an extra copy of *Hamlet* back in his tent. Did I want to read it? Maybe we could talk about it later. I said, "Don't the others read?" and he said, "Not Shakespeare." Wiry is reading *Gravity's Rainbow*, stopping every few pages to proclaim it the most important book ever written, suffering their forbearance to read long excerpts aloud at night while they're trying to fall asleep. Another, the quiet, deep one, is reading *A Fan's Notes* and occasionally he'll laugh a low gurgling chuckle without sharing the source of his mirth. The fourth guy, the one I haven't described yet, doesn't read, the English scholar said. I said, "That's like me at that age. You couldn't bribe me to crack open a book. All I wanted to do was sketch and doodle. My old man wanted me to learn to be a land surveyor like he was. Then I'd have summer work and wouldn't have to worry about money during the school year."

"My father wants me to apply to medical school," said Shakespeare Boy.

"Our fathers want only the best for us. They don't want us to suffer. They're also pretty sure we're out for their heads." The kid laughed and said we should read *Oedipus Rex* together. I asked him his name and I know he told me.

If Sylvie is making time with anybody, and I'm almost positive she isn't, it's with the fourth kid, the big blond dumb-looking one. He didn't come around to say hello the way the other three had. Can you be stupid and superior at the same time? They work all day with their shirts off and are burnt dark brown, will probably develop melanoma by the time they're forty. This buck, I must admit: shoulders on him like twin mesas. He seems to be the self-appointed wood gatherer and hewer, flailing at old gnarled stumps he finds off in the bush. Dull axe, I don't know where he found it, probably discarded somewhere.

Wiry Boy talked about how the work had changed, how last summer he humped it sixteen hours a day, running from pallet-truck to roadside grade and back. They finished both sides of the highway, at least the stretch designated to be landscaped. Perfect cascade of uniform green in a gentle slope to the shoulder, it runs two, maybe three hundred meters and then stops and the scrub takes over. If you're looking at it from the town end, it's Augusta National.

Appearance is more than the surface of objects, it's a mirror of the self, your mood, community, political reality. You landscape a section of highway so that, from where you're sitting in the Peter Pond on a Friday afternoon, well into your cups, it looks like the place where you live is the epitome of Nature tamed. No frontier hooligan place, this, no sir. Got grass. All the same kind and length. Hire a couple of kids on rider mowers to keep it looking good, they work for the same company that grows the sod, lays it, waters it, feeds it, keeps the cinch bugs at bay with good clean chemicals. Same company the Four Musketeers work for. When, fact is, this town is barely carved out of the scrub. It exists for the sole purpose of extracting heavy oil from the sand underlying it. Get up here and look around sometime. Lovely little neighbourhoods sprouting all over. Got grass. Sprinklers going all the livelong day. Nothing permanent, nothing like a basement or a firm foundation. We're floating on a sea of oil-saturated sand. When the giant excavation machines finish eating their fill over yonder, they come knocking at the front door, and all the good company folk have to hoist their houses onto wheels and vamoose.

Sylvie came back from town one day with a big can of stove-black enamel and some smaller cans of different coloured latex. "What are you going to do with those, paint the house?" I said. She said, "Mind your own business, I love you, OK?" Now what was that supposed to mean except, "Don't interfere, old man. You stopped producing anything of relevance decades ago." See if I'm going to haul myself across the way, which is strewn with garbage and rocks and firewood and cooking pits. Bloody obstacle course.

By my reckoning, we should have run out of cash about a month ago. Not that our expenses are all that great. No rent, no property taxes. Food and booze and clothes and the occasional meal out. The Pond finally took the hint and installed a ramp for the artist in his chariot. I had to get Sylvie to adjust the footrests. They were too high and the left one kept falling off whenever I bumped into something. Pal Chick came up from the city with his buddy the carpenter and they built the shack for Sylvie and me out of construction site waste, perfectly fine pieces of lumber and particleboard. They made a ramp instead of steps. I can get in and out when I want, have a nice little open-air commode set up out back in a cedar clearing, easy enough to hoist myself on and off. She tried to get me to paint again by having them build me the same kind of lean-to she has. When it was finished I wheeled over and took a sniff: protection from the elements, plenty of light, work table for tools and paint. Storage shelf off to one side for Masonite and frames. Oh, a veritable dream. She looked so pleased with herself.

"Thanks," I said, "thanks awfully much."

"Should I set up your easel for you?" she said.

"That would be great."

So she did and she went away to give me some time alone and I used a can of solvent to burn the thing to the ground.

"You drink too much," said Baby Beard one day.

"No," I said, "I drink just enough." He looked so sanctimonious I wanted to kill him. "What do you study?" I wanted to say go away, it's Sunday, go to church, go to the International House of Pancakes. Why aren't you out growing grass? Why are you messing with my view of this lovely transient camp? Go build yourself a parquet shack like The Prophet over there.

"Zoology. I study frogs."

"Frogs."

"Yes. We're finding that they're disappearing at an alarming rate. They're born with so many genetic mutations that it's becoming difficult to find a normal one. Their skins are so thin and moist that they absorb the UV radiation no longer blocked by the ozone layer, in those spots where the ozone layer has holes." He smiled angelically, like he was absolving me of my sins. If I were to paint him, I'd do him in a shimmering chromatic hue, something inherently worshipful and satirical at the same time.

"You're studying what happens to frogs."

"Yes. I go into the marshes at night and collect them in a net."

"Do you use a light?"

"Yes, a low wattage flashlight."

"That's not really fair, don't you think, for the poor croaking little saps."

"Fair?"

"Not a fair fight."

"It's hardly a fight."

"Oh no? What do you do when you're finished with the slimy little peckers?"

"They're not slimy, as a matter of fact, and we release them back into the wild."

"You don't say."

Frogs. I still hear them croaking and trilling and generally raising ruckus all night, murdering sleep.

"It's not only about one species of amphibian." Prissy look of divine peace.

"Save the croaking peepers," I said, taking a sip of heaven. "What I wouldn't do for an ice cube. By any chance is one of you boys an electrical engineer who could rig me up a solar panel or a wind turbine by which I might power an icebox?"

"There's still time to save the world." Fur-faced environmentalist creep. "Why aren't you down in the swamps of the Amazon, somewhere sweet and lethal like that?"

I GET THE ITCH sometimes to slap paint onto Masonite again and see what I can scrape up. I've been thinking about where and what we are up here in northern Alberta, specks floating on a skin of rubble and vegetation on the surface of this vast ocean of heavy oil and sand. There's something here I want to capture, an idea of immensity and impermanence.

This is as good a place as any I've lived in. We stay out of each other's way for the most part. The Prophet can get tiring, but even he has something new to say occasionally. He gets his transmissions, as he calls them, from Bateson, his twenty-five-pound cat, which looks more like a lynx than a domesticated tabby. I've told him this, many's the occasion, i.e., Beware, chum, lest you wake up some night *sans* ears. Something he's been on about for a while could be said to touch on Sylvie and me. He kept repeating, "Move or be moved," just under his breath, and if I didn't known him better I'd say he had a neurological problem.

The fabulous four drag their carcasses back to the camp at the end of a twelve-hour workday. They try to make a fire, give up in the rain, hunt for the opener, apply the axe to the lid, down the beef stew cold, worm their way into their bags, don wet jeans in the morning. They go off in the dented Corolla, unwashed, bellies empty until mid-morning break when they hoof it over to the strip mall, where they get a cruller and juice, not coffee, because there's no Johnny-on-the-Spot where they're working, a pretty little subdivision of trailer homes laid out just so on streets that curve in on themselves like cochlear passages. I watch them and think, Give me a day of that, just one. Give me the sleep of the dead at the end of it. Give me the sweet ache in the thighs and back.

Wiry Boy brought Paul Bunyan over to see me the other day. Nice kid. Brian, Ben, Bobby. Why can't I make it stick? He's not in school. Wants to make enough to winter-over in Whistler. He's some kind of Olympic god, this blond mesomorph. Men and women must swoon in equal numbers in his presence. Robert Redford with smoother skin. I see the camera adoring this specimen. I would never paint someone like him, though, me on my portrait musings again. Why bother? The camera would capture everything there was to net. It's all on the surface. Unless. Unless we're going to concentrate on the eyes, which are so faint a watery blue that you expect to see angelfish swimming through pink coral at the bottom of a long gaze into them.

They were taking the day off, their first in a month, because they were tired like pig iron and the day's lost wages weren't worth their getting sick. I turned the chair so that they could sit on the rail across my little porch. It was a good day to stay home, the sun warming the clearing, the puddles from the night's rain shrinking as we talked. I told them to go inside and fire up the Coleman for coffee, if they wanted. Mosquitoes danced on the verge of the clearing, just out of the sun. Snores escaped from a van with Newfoundland plates that had driven into camp the night before, the Prophet emerging from his parquet mosque long enough to greet them and to recite his Hammurabi's Code of camp rules, which everybody ignored, and to demand an entry fee of twenty dollars, which they actually paid him and which Sylvie retrieved and returned to them, informing them that we were a tax-free zone and that their only obligation was to bother no one who didn't want to be bothered.

The skier asked me how I became wheelchair bound, divining, I suppose, from the look of my legs, that the accident had been fairly recent. I gave him the briefest of accounts: work accident, snapped steel cable, wrong place wrong time. God caught snoozing. God in a bitchy mood, more likely. They were perceptive enough to see that it was the last thing I wanted to talk about, and switched the talk to their own work experience. They told me about an incident involving their boss, a bull who with his teeth pulled buses chained together. Something about the black plastic pipe they connect to fire hydrants for irrigation. "Giv 'er," they kept saying in imitation of the man, "giv 'er."

After a lull the lumberjack said, "Sylvie's getting a good price for your paintings. She's really pleased."

"Excuse me?"

"The dealer from Edmonton. He comes up once a week, buys everything she shows him. I took art history last year and we covered you and the Bras D'Or Lake group. You guys were huge. Shows in Montreal, Atlanta, Tokyo. Man. That was like early Sixties, right?"

So.

Art history. Wait long enough and you get covered.

I wonder what she's using as a scoring instrument. Not everything works equally well. I threw all my tools away, so I'm curious. A pin or sewing needle is too fine, a knitting needle to big and blunt. I found that a tiny screwdriver set, the kind used to fix watches and eyeglasses and the like, gave me the precise line I needed, the different heads producing a variation in the final effect as the layers would be revealed. I can't remember if I showed her that set. I must have. I used a fishhook for one of the paintings. A dinner fork for another. The saw blade on my Swiss Army knife. She can use whatever she wants.

The least she can do is get it right. Her dealer is either an ignoramus, a con artist himself or somebody who's been duped by extraordinary talent. How to find out? I could ask her when she comes in for supper. "Hey, Sylvie, did you let the enamel dry well enough before you started scraping?" Something subtle like that. "Did you press more heavily in the centre than toward the edges, to give the effect of a light source emanating from the middle?"

"Oh, yes, Bill, I did. And I made each stroke one fluid motion with no stopping, to avoid smearing and smudging."

Just kill me now.

It's not simply a matter of imitation. If she's going to do this right she has to take the work to the next level. But where exactly is that? Where was I headed before I fell on my face? Something interesting was happening with the vertical zip in *Dream of Flux*. The slight curve gives it an anti-geometric quality and the eye is drawn into the surface, not simply onto and across it. I could tell her that. Maybe I already have. She's a good student, sharp. If anyone can pull it off, Sylvie can. Depth, the sensation of texture and depth in the two-dimensional image. Hold the eye fast to a single spot and invite—no, compel it to stay until it has travelled deep into the work. Possess the eye of the beholder and refuse to relinquish it until it has been seduced and cleansed. The eye and the mind must not retreat from the work before the beholder has been fundamentally changed.

She knows that. We've talked about it. When the viewer speaks, the artwork has to answer, understandably or not. Otherwise it's a failure.

So many failures. So many fires. If I were a stronger man I would stop her. So much is stacked in teetering columns against her. She should stop now. She should scram, head for firmer ground.

MY FUTURE IN INSURANCE

MY FUTURE
IN INSURANCE

◭

Eileen was more curious about the letter than John was, although it was addressed to him. Neither of them recognized the return address. "Don't open it or anything," she said.

It was laser-printed on heavy bright bond, the text attractively set between wide margins. He recognized the template the writer had chosen. Junior Executive. It gave the impression that the writer cared about the tidiness and clarity of the presentation but didn't want to be thought stiff or stuffy. The sender's name, Wahid Rapinder, and his telephone number and mailing and e-mail addresses were printed in a youthful calligraphy font; the texture of the strokes looked as if they had been painted by hand only moments before.

Dear Mr. Merton,

I was given your name by our mutual friend, Ben Sharma, who assured me that should I ever want to get into the insurance game, you would be the one to contact, given your considerable knowledge of the ins and outs of the industry.

To this end I would dearly appreciate any pointers you might provide me. I recently graduated from Sheridan College in a related field, Medical Records, but have no desire to pursue it as a career, because I have come to believe that patient confidentiality is too easily compromised under the present system. But during the course of my studies I did learn something about the nature of insurance, and came to believe in that for which it stands. I refer, of course, to the matter of personal and community security provided by our great insurance companies, a.k.a., peace of mind, something I think we can all appreciate.

I know I would make a first-rate insurance adjustor, given my superior analytical mind and my passion for justice. Too many people think they can steal from the great insurance companies with impunity. Not I. As far as I am concerned, a deductible is there for a reason, and I for one would never submit a false claim simply because I thought it was my right. A gentleman of your experience and stature in the business world would agree with me on that point, I trust.

I would most emphatically like to meet with you to discuss this matter, a.k.a., my future in insurance. I have read about your company and consider it to be one of, if not *the* best when stacked up against the competition. Please don't read anything more into that statement than there is. I'm the last person I know who would engage in the despicable act of buttering a person on both sides, you least of all. Rather, my motive in undertaking the aforementioned research was simply to arm myself with the most up-to-date information I could as I launch myself wholeheartedly into the exciting world of work. I hope you appreciate what I mean by that. Surely you remember what it was like to be twenty-two and drowning in ideas but lacking practical experience. At least, at the risk of insulting you, I hope you haven't distanced yourself so far in years and attitude that you cannot empathize with a young man in my situation.

The letter ran to a third page, where it dwindled in repetitious obsequiousness.

He looked up at Eileen, who had been reading over his shoulder. "He thinks I'm some sort of company star. What's Sharma thinking, sending him to me?"

Merton wrote Parity Mutual's monthly newsletter and the quarterly and annual reports. Ben Sharma worked down in investments. They had met when John wrote a profile of him. Sharma was easy to talk to and fun to have at a party. He was the kind of man you didn't miss when he wasn't around but who made the moment pleasant. "I don't know how I'm supposed to help this young friend of his." Wahid Rapinder, he thought, you have the wrong man. What can I possibly give you? How he'd found Merton's home address, and why he hadn't sent the letter in care of the office, bothered him less than did the young man's erroneous assumption that Merton was someone who could open doors for him. He looked at the first page again. Medical record keeping. Now there was a worthwhile pursuit. The boy was an idealist, as one should be at his age. He didn't want to serve Big Brother. He wrote well enough for the business world, was perhaps trying too hard to sound formal, but his priorities seemed solid.

"Why don't you meet him? He sounds nice, and he's gone out of his way to find you."

"Why should I?"

"He's looking for help. Reassurance."

"Nobody gave me a leg up."

"Your father got you this job! You'd still be occupying a chair at the Hug-a-Mug and gazing out the window if it hadn't been for him and his connections."

"My literary pretensions embarrassed him. His son the *boulevardier*."

"He didn't want you to starve."

"You're not serious about me meeting this kid."

"What would it hurt? You have a coffee with him, tell him what you do, maybe help him better define his goals. It's not going to kill you. Maybe he'll turn out to be a friend."

"I'm more than twice his age. What could we possibly have in common?"

"The insurance game. Demutualization. The future of the center redline. Don't be such a piddling miser."

"I'm not you. I can't just put myself out there the way you do."

As soon as he'd said it he regretted his tone. When it came to gathering material for his reports he could "put himself out there" as well as anyone. He had to talk to people and meet new faces all the time. The difference between what he and Eileen did—she was a service representative for an Internet provider—was that he got to ask the initial question. He controlled the direction an interview took.

"It'll be all right, whatever you choose to do."

Oh, I'm sunk, he thought, looking into her boundlessly optimistic brown eyes, knowing that she knew what he was going to do even before he did.

HE E-MAILED RAPINDER to say he'd be happy to meet the young man for coffee. He suggested a time on Saturday morning at a café near where he and Eileen lived.

The boy was sitting on a high stool in the front window, drinking an iced cappuccino and holding a copy of the latest Parity Mutual annual report, as he had told Merton he would be. Rather than introduce himself immediately, Merton stood at the counter pretending to decide what he would buy to drink. The choice was extensive and elaborate enough that the young woman behind the counter didn't intervene. This gave him time to glance surreptitiously at Rapinder.

He had black hair cut well, and not so short as to be severe or to accentuate facial flaws, of which there appeared to be none. He fit a culturally broad definition of handsomeness and was the type Eileen got crushes on. Merton bought a regular sized coffee; he would give the interview the time it took to drink one cup, no more.

"If you find any mistakes don't tell me about them," he said, standing close enough to Rapinder to let him know he was addressing him, but a few steps far enough away to assure him that he was non-threatening. We can talk like this, he wanted to convey. We can banter across a public space the way men who don't know each other do, about the weather, sports or the high cost of car repairs.

"Mr. Merton."

He gestured palm-out to prevent Rapinder from sliding off his stool. They shook hands and the boy tried to smile, but seemed too nervous to make it anything more than a grimace. It surprised Merton to think that he could make anyone nervous. He enjoyed it. Usually he was the one trying to stave off anxiety.

"Thank you for agreeing to meet me, sir. I appreciate you taking the time out of your busy schedule."

"You're saving me from the vacuuming. I should thank you."

Rapinder gave a more natural, appreciative smile at this. "It's kind, all the same. You wouldn't believe how many people don't have time for someone like me."

"Then they're hopelessly selfish," said Merton, feeling a smack of conscience as he remembered his initial reaction to Rapinder's request.

"Can you tell me, Mr. Merton, do you like what you do for a living?"

Don't begin with a question like that, he thought. Put the interviewee at ease first. If Merton were to answer truthfully he might send the kid away demoralized. Perhaps Rapinder really was looking for the truth. Maybe he was smart enough not to settle for just any job. In a profound sense, then, he had used the best possible opener. Everything essential followed from the answer. Do you like what you do? Does it like you back? Are you happy, stimulated, fulfilled?

"It's the rare day I feel like slitting my wrists."

Rapinder raised his eyebrows, a look of alarm registering before he recovered his composure and smiled again. "What I wrote to you, about feeling that insurance is my calling? I wasn't making that up."

"Oh, I believe you. Nobody in his right mind would make up such a thing, I'm sure. You do realize that I'm neither an investigator nor an adjustor. I don't even underwrite policies."

"You don't?"

"I assumed you knew. That report you're holding? I wrote most of that." Rapinder turned the pages as if searching for a reference. "I don't know how much help I can be to you."

The young man's smile flickered out, and when he tried to relight it Merton thought it would be better if he didn't smile at all.

"I could put you in touch with someone else in the company."

"You don't have to do that."

"Maybe I want to. Don't be so easily defeated. You know," said Merton, hearing his words skip blithely ahead of his thoughts, "if you're going to be successful in this business, you can't let minor setbacks prevent you from achieving your goals."

Merton told him that if they were to meet at his office on Monday at ten in the morning, he would show Rapinder around and introduce him to some people who could help him. Not "might" but "could." He didn't say that his office was a baffle-wall cubicle he rarely used, and which would probably be occupied by a temporary worker or filled with boxes of photocopy machine toner.

Rapinder thanked him excessively; in order to stop him, Merton steered the boy out of the coffee shop and onto the sidewalk.

"Tomorrow, then. I mean Monday, Monday morning. Ten on the nose."

"Yes, I'm looking forward to it. We'll get you connected with the right people. If you had an interest in writing, well, now, there's something I might be able to help you with."

"Really? Because I think I might like to do that, too. Write. My teachers used to say that I had a good imagination. If I can't get a job in insurance *per se*, maybe you could—"

"We'll see what happens," said Merton, feeling the loose coil of control twist and fray in his hand.

WHEN HE GOT to his desk Monday morning, he inspected the stacks of paper piled on it to make sure that they belonged to him. He cleared space for his laptop, opened it, and was trying to decide what file to pretend to be working on, when a face appeared in the doorway.

"John," said the man, and suddenly Merton saw the resemblance. Ben Sharma could have been Wahid Rapinder two decades older. They shook hands.

"Wally is thrilled to be getting this attention."

"Yes, well. No guarantees."

"I could try to find him work with me, but it would be a lot of photocopying and shredding and sitting around on his hands waiting for lunch and tea."

"He's a friend, is he?"

"Nephew, actually. My sister's youngest, the baby of the baby. Now there's a pedigree. Spoiled? Tell me about it. Those two couldn't fall out of bed without assistance. I guess this is nepotism rearing its ugly head. Guilty as charged."

"All I can do is show him around. He should talk to somebody who actually knows something about insurance."

"Are you saying that you don't know what you're doing, John? Are you telling me that those reports you write are gibberish? Because if you don't know anything about this business, you've got everybody down on Seventeen fooled. I can't speak for corporate governance, mind you, but I'd be willing to bet my job you've got those fat cats fooled, too."

"I write what people tell me. It's not difficult."

"You're much too modest. When Wally first approached me—when his mother first phoned me, actually, in tears over the uncertain future of her youngest child, begging me to do something to keep him off the street, I told her, Baby Noni, I said, leave it to me. If one man can give Wally what he needs, it's my friend John Merton. I have seen this man in action, and let me tell you, that is one very able scribe. He is just enough removed from the hubbub to see things with a clear eye. Because, face it, John Merton, our Nabokov, our Proust, our own Robertson Davies of insurance, what young stud in his early twenties has the least clue? I mean about anything. He does a course: pharmacy. Not for him. He borrows money from his family, travels to Mumbai, tries to become a Bollywood big shot, slinks home with his tail tucked behind his balls. Thinks there's nothing in this life for him. Then he meets—you guessed it—a pretty girl. She's studying to be a medical records manager, and so of course that's what he wants to be. He finds the course either too easy, too hard, or too boring, I can't remember which. Right? You're getting the picture, John, the general trend?"

Merton pursed his lips, leaned back in his chair and folded his hands behind his head. He had an idea as to what Sharma was telling him. The boy was as likely to enjoy working in insurance as he was breaking rock with a sledgehammer. Merton's contribution would be to feel him out on various parameters; his interests, beliefs, aptitudes, anything that might better help them steer "Wally" towards the right pursuit. The law. Medicine. Banking. Dumpster diving. "We'll find the right fit for him."

"I knew it. I knew you would be the man. You won't regret it. This will be good for you, too."

Yes, he was about to say when his phone buzzed and he picked up the receiver. This was what Eileen was always urging him to do. Step out beyond the palisade of his selfish concerns. Stretch. Give for no other reason but the giving itself. Get a little crazy now and then.

His visitor was downstairs waiting to be brought up. Merton thanked the receptionist and hung up the phone. When he looked up, Ben Sharma had left.

MERTON TOOK RAPINDER from department to department, floor to floor, from open arms to puzzled looks. Afterwards, he brought him down to the restaurant off the lobby, and at a table in the low-light, post-coffee-break, pre-lunch lull, he thought about what he would say next. How to convey the difficult message.

"I liked the last woman we spoke to. She was very helpful."

"Linda."

"Yes. I could work with her."

"*For* her. VP Sales, remember? She's the type who smiles in your face and makes cooing sounds while she eviscerates you."

"Whoa."

"She's not that bad."

"Some people didn't seem to know why we were there. That's okay, though. I still learned a lot. I have a much better sense of how the business works."

"Good. You can tell me." That made Rapinder laugh. "You still think this is what you want to do?"

"Oh, definitely."

Merton was preparing the blow—you're not cut out for this, Wally, it takes a hard head and a harder heart, you have to be tough, as tenacious as a terrier—when a man and woman came in and sat in a nearby booth. He could see the back of part of the woman's left shoulder. He was sure it was Eileen.

"Tell me more about what you do, John. I think it would be chill to write all day and get paid for it."

"It's not as glamorous as you think." What was she doing here? Her office was a forty-minute subway and bus ride away. "I spend most of my time..." She was checking up on him. It didn't make any sense. Who was the man? He knew all the people she worked with.

"Most of your time?"

"Gathering."

"Gathering's awesome."

What was going on?

"So, do you, like, need an assistant or anything?"

"A what?"

"I was thinking researcher, somebody to go out and get all the information and bring it back to you to write up."

He was going to have to go over there. No way around it. She was on his turf, as it were, not that he spent enough time in the building to be considered a holder of turf there. It wouldn't do to wait until the evening, while they were reading the mail and unwinding with a drink, to ask, "By the way, did I happen to see you in Giorgio's today? Long way from Scarberia, hmm?"

"I don't have enough work to keep me busy full time, if you want to know the truth."

"That's cool." If Rapinder was crestfallen he was keeping his disappointment hidden. His tone remained cheerful. He looked around the room as if thinking that he might like to work there as a waiter.

"Would you excuse me a moment? I think I know those people."

When Merton stood and took a few steps towards the booth where the couple was sitting, he saw that it wasn't Eileen after all, only someone who resembled her closely from behind. The question now was what to do. Should he return to Rapinder, sit, admit his mistake? That would be the intelligent thing to do. But he had run out of things to say to the too-pleasant, too-eager young man. Merton's heart was no longer in the enterprise, this leading by hand, this being a guide, advisor, cheerleader. He wanted to close his eyes, open them and see that the boy had disappeared.

He walked over to the booth where Eileen's look-alike sat. "Would you mind if I stood here a minute?" he said, looking from the man to the woman and back.

"Excuse me?" she said.

"I know it sounds odd—we don't know each other—but the young man I'm sitting with—that's him over there." Merton turned and gave Rapinder a brief wave. "He thinks I have a job for him."

"And of course you don't." The woman was just barely keeping her impatience in check. She was not in the least like Eileen.

"I don't know what to say to him."

"Just tell him the truth," she said.

"If it helps to talk about—" said the man.

"I'm sure this gentleman can handle the situation without our interference, Ted."

"Hey, listen, you've been good enough to let me stop here and collect my thoughts."

Merton was about to step away when he felt a presence at his elbow.

"Everything okay?"

"Fine, fine. This is Wahid. Wahid, this is Ted and—I'm sorry."

"Jennifer," said the woman icily.

"Call me Wally, please. Hi. Hi there. How's it going?" He reached over to shake their hands.

"Fine," said Jennifer. "I think your friend here has something important to tell you, Wally."

She picked up a legal-size envelope and pushed it into her briefcase.

"We were going to sign those," said Ted.

"I've signed them." She withdrew the envelope and practically threw it across the table.

"Jen."

"Sign them and give them back to Paul."

"This wasn't the way. . ."

"There's no *way*, Ted. There's never been a way."

"I thought we could do this as friends."

"Are you two, like, splitting up?"

Merton cleared his throat and sent Rapinder a cautionary glance.

"Perceptive young man," said Jennifer.

"How long were you guys together?"

"Seven years. Technically we're still married," said Ted, forming the envelope and its contents into a cylinder and peering through it at the floor.

"We really should go," said Merton, gesturing to his protégé.

"Can't you sit awhile?" said Ted. "What do you have to rush off to?"

Jennifer's eyes flicked up to meet Merton's, and darted away. She looked angry, bewildered and vulnerable, as if the men knew a secret set of rules she didn't. It was like that game: I like steel, but I don't like iron. I like oysters, but I don't like eggs. On you go like that, declaring your strange pairs of likes and dislikes until somebody discovers the key to the pattern.

"I'm leaving," she said.

"What do we have to rush off to, John?" said Rapinder. "Here, scooch over." He and Merton slid in beside the couple, hemming them in, Rapinder on Ted's side and Merton on Jennifer's.

"Oh no, I'm not staying," she said. "Ted?"

"Yes?"

She made a fricative sound as she picked up her purse and bumped against Merton with her elbow and shoulder. He stood to let her out.

"So, you have something important to tell me, John?" said Rapinder after she was gone.

"Oh, it's . . . not important."

"I hear you're looking for work," said Ted. "What's your thing?"

"John's been showing me the insurance business." Wally listed his qualifications and aspirations.

"Medical records. Really. You know your way around an EMR package? Billing, appointments, coding, insurance claims, all that?"

"I know the basics."

"We're in the building, a small clinic, three MDs. We lost our receptionist and records keeper a year ago. You just met her. Some people lose one or the other; me, I lose a spouse and a prized employee at the same time. We've been limping along with temps. Do you have a copy of your cv?"

Rapinder patted his shirt pocket. "Flash key."

"Why don't you come up and have a look? We can print you out, introduce you to the other doctors."

MERTON REMAINED SEATED in the booth. The waitress appeared and poured him a cup of coffee. That giddy feeling, the offspring of surprise and relief, subsided and was replaced by deflation. The boy had excused himself, going so far as to beg Merton's permission to leave.

"Are you sure it's all right, John?"

"Are you kidding? Go! By all means. How often do you get a chance like this?"

But there had been moments during the introductions upstairs, as he was guiding the young man from one department of Parity Mutual to the next, when he had felt a mad urge to turn to him and say, "You can have my job. Yes, it's true, I mean it. I've been thinking about changing careers. No, I'm not joking. It's yours."

When he told Eileen about it later that evening her eyes got damp, though she was still smiling, teasing him about being upstaged as an altruist and mentor.

"I would never give my job away. You don't have to worry."

"I know that," she said. "But you wanted to."

"Yes, I suppose there's that."

"I'm sorry, John."

"Don't be."

"You did a good thing today. If you hadn't answered his letter, he'd still be looking for work."

He accepted the compliment just as he accepted her embrace, letting it knead the knots of his sadness. No one understood him the way she did. If he were writing a story it would never end like this, with a woman comforting her husband, reminding him of his virtues, accommodating his gilt-edged wounds. Yet he could think of no better ending to the day.

IN THE WASH

IN THE WASH

▲

Miss Pretty looked perplexed as she stood outside the Fold and Sort, rattling the handle of the glass door. Usually all she had to do was pull up in her white Miata, honk, and Jameer would run outside to take her bag. Whenever he daydreamed about her, he pictured her driving around in that little two-seater, circulating like a leukocyte through the arteries of the impure city. It was the kind of vehicle he would have scoffed at had one of his sons been driving it, but dressing her it was an extension of her beauty.

He rushed from the rear of the laundromat to unlock and open the front door. He said sorry so many times in a row that she said, "Don't worry about it. Not a problem," accentuating the first syllable in "problem." It was as if she were absolving him of sin, including his adoration, which he could not suppress. He gave no one else the level of attention he gave Miss Pretty. No one else looked like this, her hair a confection of captured light, her dark wool suit beguilingly tight.

She had delicates, whites, knits, darks, and light-coloured items requiring cold water, five loads she never separated herself. "That's what I'm paying you for, right, J'meer?" He thought about her abbreviated delicates, then about his wife's not so delicate and so much more substantial underclothing, which was durable, cotton, and easy to clean.

He logged her work order, trying to think of something to say to delay her departure. She smiled and said goodbye over her shoulder as the North Wind, concierge, opened the door for her. Something in the ceiling made a cracking sound. He shivered as he watched her drive, all snowy, away. He was turning the key in the door to hold it fast again when the phone trilled, the first of a series.

"Yes we are open."

"Yes we are drop-off."

"We are closed at nine o'clock tonight. The last load must be in by eight fifteen."

"Five dollars each load. No, no bleach, if that is your wish. Your desire is not to be bleached. I understand."

Then the middle son, Khaled, who had already phoned three times that morning.

"No. No more money. I have no money."

"Hello? That is your problem. I do not take the taxi. You know what time the bus comes. That is not my problem. No. Goodbye."

"Fold and Sort. No, I cannot. If you were to wake yourself in time you would not always be missing the bus. Yes, you will be late, most assuredly. I will tell her. That you will not be there in time. No. No. That is for you to explain. I am not the one who stays out all night like the cat."

He looked down. Over the day's newspaper, which lay spread on the counter, his hands became claws, hovering, throttling empty air. He felt his face tighten. Here a young Muslim woman had written that every unclad whore in a recent beauty contest was fit to be one of the Prophet's brides. Why did people write such blasphemy? He had not yet had time to pray.

He folded *The Chronicle-Herald* and stowed it under the counter. A confused growl escaped from his throat. Two customers, sour-looking older men, glanced up from their magazines. They had been standing outside waiting for him to open the business, sighing, making him feel rushed as he went about the room, turning on lights, thrusting quarters into dryers to warm them, doing a quick sweep of the washing machines to see that the woman who worked evenings had left them clean and empty. If he could find ten minutes to recite from his prayer book, he might find momentary peace, preparation for the day, blessed forgetfulness.

When Jameer looked up from his seat behind the counter, the landlord, Gould, was standing on the other side. The man was at least twenty years older than most when they retired, and he showed no sign of deceleration. Jameer stood.

"Hello, how are you, sir?"

"My property-tax bill is thirty-two percent higher than last year's. My insurance is up almost twice that. I'm going in for a hernia operation, into that charnel house they call a hospital. My grandson the lawyer wants me to hand over the business to him and move to Orlando. After I deal with you I am going to a meeting at Beth Israel to discuss the latest desecration of headstones in our cemetery. I'm fine, thank you. Who am I to complain?"

"It is a terrible thing."

"What, that I am alive? That I have enough to eat?"

"No, about the headstones."

"The broken ones can be replaced. There is such a thing as cleanser. Don't concern yourself about it, Aswari. Now what is this about the heat? They are freezing, these good people?" he said, glancing over his shoulder. "The pipes have burst? Where is the flood, then?"

Jameer looked at him and hesitated, almost did not say anything. Unless all the dryers were running full-blast for an hour, the place never got warm enough to allow him to remove his coat and hat, a plaid insulated hunting cap with quilted earmuffs. Gould didn't seem to feel the cold. Perhaps he was already dead. How was it possible to fight such a man? Jameer wanted to show him how the wind blew the door open. How had Gould gotten inside? He must have used his own key. The heart of the world was freezing into a solid cube of impenetrable ice, the door would not stay closed unless it was locked from the inside, and in front of the dryers the ceiling beam sagged precariously. One of these days it was going to crash down on his head, squash him like a cockroach flattened by a boot heel, and he only hoped Gould would be there to see it happen. God certainly would.

"Just turn up the thermostat."

"I cannot afford to burn more fuel in that manner, Mr. Gould, unlike yourself."

"You think it's dripping off me! You see me flying to Saint-Tropez for the winter? You see that car out there? Nine years old. This is the same overcoat I wore to my son's bris."

Jameer looked outside. His moustache bristled painfully as if it were growing inward. The Mercedes sedan parked there was worth more money than Jameer's entire business.

"I will have to let something go, pay less rent, the price of oil…"

The old man leaned into the counter. Jameer felt it move toward him and he took a half step back. "Do you know how quickly I could replace you in this space? Two days. Businessmen are lined up waiting to take your place."

"Please, I am only saying—"

"Do I care what you are saying? You want to bring me to my knees."

"The door…"

"You're throwing me out now!"

"No, the door, it will not, I am telling you, remain closed. The very coldest air…"

"And the weather is now my fault!"

Jameer came out from behind the counter, moved past the old man, passing behind him, and went to the door. He turned the key, removed it, pulled the door open slightly and let it close.

"You *are* telling me to get out. History repeats itself."

Jameer waited. His intention had been merely to let the wind demonstrate the door's deficiency, but now that Gould had allowed the thought, and now that Jameer's anger, which he could not show, was high banked and radiant, he said nothing.

Gould raised his chin and made a quick dismissive gesture with his hand. "I want you out in ten days. You will receive a letter from the lawyer."

Jameer was too cold and tired to plead or cajole. Let the wind blow, he willed. The disobedient door remained motionless until the old man opened it and passed through.

Jameer watched him shuffle with wilful steadiness down the icy steps onto the salt-gritty sidewalk, down the nearest driveway entrance onto the narrowed street, back to the spot where his car was parked in defiance of the parking meter, which stood buried to its chin in snow and showed no paid time remaining. A man like that, thought Jameer, searching for the appropriate completion. A man like that strides the world on colossal legs. No one defeats such a creature, he defeats himself. If I picture him when I pray, perhaps my desire will focus and grow. I need my enemy. He has hurled the first spear and I embrace it, even as it pierces my body. I admire my despised foe and my love hardens me as the kiln hardens clay.

JAMEER WAITED THREE days before calling Gould's business number. It was enough time for an eviction letter, if it were on its way, to have arrived.

The phone rang five times. A youthful, unctuous, recorded voice instructed him to leave a detailed message. This was Eddie, "the lawyer," whose threatening power his grandfather evoked in the presence of truculent tenants and combative competitors.

"Please hello, Mr. Gould, this is Jameer. Dear venerable senior sir, I am calling speaking about our previous conversation, in which I believe it was a misunderstanding of my own creation. Allow me, please, to indicate to you that I am sorry and that I will deal with the heating problem according to my own steam."

WHEN HE SAW Miss Pretty next, later that morning, he was not immediately aware of her presence. He was trying to ignore an incessant car alarm when the telephone rang and he answered in Urdu, angrily because he assumed it was Khaled continuing to demand help clearing the balance of yet another maxed-out credit card.

"J'meer, I can't sit out here all day. Are you like deaf?"

"Who is this, please?"

"Look outside. I've been honking for you."

He stepped out and received her small black net bag. Before her window closed again he noticed the bruising around her right eye and the cracked puffy upper lip.

"You are well?"

She opened the window again. "I need it by four today. Can you do that?"

"Five o'clock."

"Four thirty?"

"Yes, very well, it will be all done at that time."

"You might have to pre-soak some of it first. Cold water. The dreaded visitor."

"Not at all. You are most welcome anytime."

"No, it's … never mind. You'll see."

"You would like perhaps to come inside? It is warmer there. I will make tea."

"That's sweet of you, J'meer. Things to do, you know how it is. Maybe later?"

"Please, I am somewhat anxiety ridden. About your face. Specifically."

"My face and a toad's backside."

"Excuse me please?"

"A match. It's a joke. Didn't you ever slip on the soap and fall flat on your kisser?"

"Yes. No not really."

"Yes, no, not really. You're a funny little guy. Fang says you're the only honest … we'll see you this aft, okay?" She drew her seat belt across her chest and fastened it. "Don't worry. I mean, God, smile already. Geez."

Jameer almost groaned. He had a vision: a faceless, hulking lout abrading Miss Pretty's face with the back of his hand. Justice! How to avenge this. He pictured himself, sword in hand, the beast's severed head at his feet, the gushing fount. But the faces of women, did they not provoke as much as inspire? Oh, I am the victim of deep bedevilment, he thought.

AT FOUR FORTY-FIVE Jameer was unlocking the door for two young women and a slight, pale young man, beauticians from the day spa around the corner, when sable-clad Eddie Gould entered the Fold and Sort behind them. The spa staff immediately filled eight empty washers with mud caked white towels, and fed the machines coins from a margarine tub. The boy volunteered to stay and the girls returned to work. Jameer watched Eddie watch the kid sit, pick up a thick fashion-magazine, cross his legs tightly at the crotch, hook the foot of one behind the calf of the other, and flip backwards through the surreal pages.

"It's a puzzling world," said Eddie in such a way that Jameer knew he was being addressed while Gould continued to stare at the heavily made-up boy.

"I have always thought so," said Jameer with a shiver.

The young man met Eddie's gaze. "Help you with something, Sweet Bun?"

Eddie blushed, turned and walked closer to the counter. "You got some things of Trish's to pick up."

"I am sorry?"

"Trish Myers. Small bag, black. Not a big load. Like so," he said, making the approximate size with his hands.

It took Jameer a long moment before he understood. Trish. He sounded the name in his head, wondering whether or not he would be able to say it successfully. On the masking tape by which he identified clients' loads, he always wrote "Miss P."

"Yes, it is here." He reached into a cubbyhole below the counter.

"So, you had a run-in with the old man the other day."

"It was nothing. The problem is solved."

"He never means it. Don't worry. What do I owe you?"

"No charge."

"Really? You're a prince. Deduct it from your rent. I mean that."

Jameer did not mean to laugh, but he was filling quickly with ticklish venom. Eddie chuckled, too, though uneasily. Jameer opened his mouth wide, made a booming sound. He showed Eddie his teeth. He looked at a pulsing spot on the lawyer's neck.

Soon I will be giving you my notice, he thought, still laughing. Fang.

"We'll fix that door for you."

"That would be most conducive. I thank you appreciatively."

Jameer wondered if this man would live as long as his grandfather had. He doubted it. Eddie was too soft and volatile. He let himself flail and care, cause hurt and be wounded. Unlike his grandfather, he still believed in the possibility of a better life. He had transformed a beautiful woman into a fool and a harlot in exchange for his regard. He made empty promises.

After Eddie left, the door banged open and shut repeatedly. Jameer ignored it.

He would have to announce the coming change. When? Before the end of winter, certainly. They would most likely have to move to another city. He had Toronto in mind. His wife and sons would register disbelief and alarm in predictable measure. Many long-distance phone calls would be placed, to his wife's cousin in Markham, Ontario, his parents in Rawalpindi. A man was never alone in matters as momentous as these, and for that he was thankful.

FOLLY GO NIGHTLY

BLUEBIRD

△

"HAIR APPARENT. How may I direct your call?"

"There's only the one line, Anthony," said Vera as she tried to squeeze past him, but he was blocking her with the phone cord and his body. In a hibiscus-red Don Ho tent, sand-coloured chinos and rubber flip-flops, hair wet but clean, face smooth, he looked better than usual, which some days had been the rough side of a used scouring pad, but his breath was still cherry brandy and burnt onions. She had hoped to avoid him, this.

She patted his tummy. "When are we due, little mum?"

"You're not allowed back here anymore. No, Mrs. Fenneman, that's the last thing I would say to you, dear. *Mercy sake, girl!* Rinse and set, your usual time on Wednesday. *Vera. Ve-ra. Git!"*

She shouldered her way past, stretching the spiral snake over her head. "Where does she keep them?" She rummaged under some invoices stacked on top of an unopened cardboard box. The receptionist, Angelique, she of the Shakira hair, was next door at Phil's, sucking back iced cappuccino and filtered smoke. Peeking in on her way past, Vera had seen her squinting in a booth by the window, her nose almost touching the page of her Jilly Cooper. When she still worked at the salon, Vera had vowed she would take the girl to the optometrist, but then Dr. Mem had descended with his offer and—snap—Scene the Next. It would be so much easier to go across and ask Angelique to come dig out Vera's final paycheque than have to endure another minute of Twister with Anthony.

"Not your usual time? *Get OUT of there, please.* That is not a problem, love, we will unsheathe our trusty eraser and hmmmdoodleedum, presto-changeo, voilà, ten-thirty it is. Done. Yes. Uh-huh. *She already sent it out in the mail.* Okay, bye then, Mrs. Eff. *If you don't mind.* Until then, then. Oh, moi aussi. *Go away, defector.* Half-mast, I mean PAST, that's correct. See you then, my dear." He hung up.

"Tippler," she said. "Stutterer."

"Round heel. Follicle floozie. *Lollipop? 'Who loves you, baby?'* I could expire right here from derisive laughter. Buh-hwaw!"

"Booze fish. Scissor bitch. Don't talk to me about licking lollies. Furthermore, I don't believe you. She told me she'd hold onto it. Now where … is … it … hoho!" The cash register drawer yielded to the old code. After all, it had only been a month since she'd quit, and they knew where to find her. She wanted to scrutinize the cheque to make sure Berlin Barbara had tacked on vacation pay. Later, she decided. Escape was her more immediate need.

"We've missed you," said Anthony when the counter was again solidly between them.

"No you didn't, but thank you for the sediment."

"Barbie cried when she was making up your EI sheet. We had some great gabs, didn't we?"

"I don't remember Frau Barbarella actually ever speaking to you."

"You and I, silly. Old chair neighbours. I used to watch you out of the corner of my eye, copy little snippets of your technique. Sigh."

"I never knew that, Anthony. How touching. To think that you could turn workplace theft into something so schmaltzy."

"And guess what else, Little Miss Reforestation? Guess who's back in town? You'll never, not in one trillion eons."

"Don't. I shouldn't even be down here right now."

"You're telling me."

"I mean we're over-booked, we made the news anchor's plugs too big, and he's coming in today sometime for an unscheduled consult. Not sure about the symmetry or something. Thinks his hairline is going to fuse with his eyebrows. It's only been a week. You haven't told anybody, have you? Confidential. Anyway. So, who is it?"

"First Base. Nyuk-nyuk."

"Anthony! Just don't. I'm going away now. Say hello to Madam Mengele for me, the witch. The nerve, suggesting I sign up for refresher courses."

"It's your *bon ami, je pense,* your Hello Spicky."

"Huh?"

The phone rang. Anthony gave her an ambiguous hand wave as he took the call. The gesture might have meant, "Stay and all will be divulged" or "Time's up, sucka, thanks for playing our nostalgia game today. Come on back to us real real soon."

She shook her head. Could it really be Jaime? Anthony had never met him, but after Vera told him the story of her first crush he begged her to tell it again and again. "I can't quite picture him yet. I can taste him, though: hazelnut. Yum. Leave nothing out. Does he have long lashes? Fillings? If they're metal, don't say."

Still mulling, she went outside and around to the window where Angelique was sitting. When she tapped, the girl startled, a full-body quake, and dropped her book. Vera plastered the cheque against the glass, mouthed a thank-you, and left her lips in red on the pane. Angelique smiled, indicated that she was coming outside for a hug. Vera waved her off. No time. She had to get back upstairs to the seedling factory. *Later: you and me. Umbrella drinks soon-soon at the Folly. Mega chick-chat. Babes only, you bet.*

Doctor Mahmoud Memviziri was in his office when she returned, his door shut. She stowed her purse in her desk and went back out into the reception area to meet her next appointment.

"Sarah Emberley?"

The younger of two women stood and said, "Sally." They shook hands. She was dressed in a smart charcoal-coloured business suit with matching hose and a puff of red and yellow at the neck. The makeup was understated, the hair, predictably magnificent, like oiled teak. The other looked up expectantly. Vera recognized the old girl's halo of white spun sugar: Barbara's eleven o'clock Tuesday.

"Why don't you both come in?" said Vera, anticipating their question. "Sometimes this calls for a second pair of eyes."

She sat them down and explained the procedure.

"Today all I'm going to do is take some pictures, front, back and side. I'll refer to these while I make your wig."

"Oh," said Sally, "I was hoping…"

"She has her first treatment tomorrow."

Vera smiled. She understood. The sooner the better, then. "First round, you might get away with little or no loss at all," but she saw the waning resolve in the younger woman's eyes: do it now or not ever.

After taking three quick Polaroids, Vera led her to the sink, covered her from the neck down with a smock and tilted her back in the chair. The warm spray turned the thick hair into an almost black, solid-looking mat. She cleaned it with a light shampoo and applied a conditioner and sealant that would help keep the colour from fading. She squeezed excess water into a towel and led her to a chair, where she combed out the kinks and knots. With a pair of scissors she began to cut close to the scalp. The doctor had suggested, only once, that she might work quicker with electric clippers. "I am not shearing sheep here. Do I tell you how to plant saplings?" she said.

Normally Vera did not bring out the mirror until after the client had chosen an interim wig, but this one wanted to see herself shorn.

"Maybe I'll just go with this," she said. "The new me. What do you say, Mum? Warrior Sal, ready for the fray."

"Once more into the breach," said Mum with goofy enthusiasm.

Vera told her that even this spiky half-inch was going to fall out. Some women made do with scarves or soft floppy hats. "Let me show you some before-and-afters." She brought out a photo album and let them flip through the pages showing former clients. They had to look closely to see a difference between the growing hair and Vera's custom-made wigs.

"How many of these women are still alive?"

Vera winced. "Every single one of them, of course. That's your one allowable dumb question."

She brought out three synthetic wigs that were close in colour and length to Sally's hair. She tried one on, walked over to the portable full-length mirror, frowned. "Can you make me a blonde? I was thinking slutty porn queen."

"Oh, Sally," said Mum.

"I'll get my nails done. Then I'll stop at that tacky lingerie shop and buy something wicked. Champagne, of course. Pick up a naughty flick. He'll think he's having an affair."

Vera handed them a box of facial tissues and went into the storage room. She came back with a Sharon Stone Special. The woman tried it on, guffawed, then began to cry again. She took it off, raked her fingers through what was left of her original hair, donned the wig, and tried to be the femme fatale again.

"Remember," said Vera. "Temporary. In two weeks' time, you'll look like this again," and she held up the front-view photo.

"What if the gentleman, as they say, prefers me this way? I know, don't tell me: the miracle of dye. You probably charge extra for that."

"Darn tooting," said Vera.

She even had the mother laughing by the time they left. Vera was exhausted. The anchorman was still to come. Some day, she decided, she would switch with Dr. Mem. Just for a day. He could mop up after weepy Rapunzels and she could merrily punch holes in men's scalps.

He opened his door and looked out. "All clear," she said. *Coward.*

"I was thinking that we should produce another advertisement."

Lord, please, no. Anything else. "Really?"

"Yes. The first one, to my mind, is not dignified enough."

"Dignified."

"Precisely. Let us review. Come." He led the way into his office, where he turned on a video screen and hit Play. There they were in trench coats and fedoras, she mugging in the background. What were they thinking? It had been her idea. "*Inspector Theo Kojak. I am not familiar with this television character. You say he is respectable?*" She had thought of having him try Patrick Stewart's Jean-Luc Picard or Yul Brenner's King of Siam, but this seemed easiest. It had a punch line.

The coaching had been excruciating. "*Yuh. Say, yuh. Who loves yuh, baby?*"

"Who loaves yah, bebbe."

"Try it again. *Luvs. Uh* not *oh.*"

"Looves."

He had enjoyed the lollipop once he learned how to speak with it stuck in the side of his mouth and doming the cheek. "Hey, bald men. Lissen-op. Who luffs you, baybee? Jesus, nobody. Mebbee yo momma."

"Cut! *Mommy*, Doctor. It's not gangsta rap. *Maybe your mommy.*"

The videographer, Barbara's fourteen-year-old son, recorded the doctor's spiel, but said nothing. He wouldn't have known Telly Savalas from Busby Berkeley. They shot three takes at Vera's insistence.

The doctor turned off the tape. "It is my sense that this does not come across with the necessary…"

"Gravity?"

"Precisely. I was thinking that we might ask Mr. Donnelley for his endorsement. In exchange for a price reduction."

"We'd have to wait till he grows in."

"Not absolutely. This medium is—how do you say? Frangible?" They were on Chapter Four of *Word Power Made Easy*.

"Malleable."

"We can manipulate the image, no? As we do the scalp. Yes, it is correct, I believe. I suggest some … flagellate."

That stumped her.

"Coverment. For hiding the unmentionables."

"Ah, camouflage," her department. Sure, she thought. She could work up a bit of a temporary pelt for the talking head. She wasn't convinced that Donnelley Down and Dirty at Five-Thirty would agree to lend his foursquare face to their cause. Dr. Mem was assuming that the newsreader wouldn't care that the viewing public would know about his "enhancement." As if they wouldn't be able to tell from watching his first broadcast back from "vacation."

She heard her phone and went out to her desk to answer it. "A Mr. Alexander?" said the receptionist who coordinated traffic for the four practitioners—dentist, skin specialist, podiatrist and paediatrician—who shared the second floor with Doctor Mem. "No reservation. Says he knows you?"

Vera felt a bird's wings beating in her chest. *That's Alessandro, you cow.* In the background he was la-la-ing loudly the tune to 'White Cliffs of Dover.' "Thank you, Billie. Be right there." She fixed her lipstick and passed a brush through her hair before stepping out.

Five years fell away. He was wearing sandals, tight black leather pants and a white linen shirt tied at the navel. Rings in both eyebrows, diamond chips following the curve of the tops of the ears, and those cheekbones— Mother of Angels! You could suffer a paper cut on them. He'd been in the sun, this was no light-box tan. Completely waxed from hairline to toe. Sloughed and buffed and pumped. Botoxed, too, from the look of it. She wanted to pick him up and put him under glass. Then the smile and she was whimpering, squeaking. Their hug was superfluous, the air between them a supercharged embrace.

She gave him two on each cheek and a hard slap for having dropped off the planet without sending back word one.

"Forgive me?" he said. "Are you still my bluebird? My Vera Lynn." He held out a garment bag on a hanger. "Something for tonight."

She unzipped it and lifted out a confection in pink.

"I guessed at your size. Pretty close, I think." She drew out matching pumps from the bottom of the bag.

"What do you mean, tonight?"

"I'm at Folly Go Nightly. Headlining, actually. Blush. Can you believe?"

"Jaime!" She pronounced it the way he did, "Hay-me." In high school the girls would follow him around, saying things like, "Jaime, you slay me."

"I have so much to tell you, but I'm late for rehearsal. You can come?"

"Of course I can!'

"Bring everybody you know. I want so many people crammed in there the fire marshal shuts us down." He took her cell phone number.

The door closed. Had she hallucinated? She inspected the dress, which looked familiar. It had no tag. He had come home after five years away, who knows where, and thinking of her had sat down at his mother's Singer and stitched this from memory. Because he had promised he would.

SHE WAS WORKING at Fabricland, her senior year of high school. It wasn't as many as five years ago, surely. Impossible. But yes.

He was the new boy that year. He had cocoa-butter skin. Whenever he smiled, all she saw were killer brown eyes and Chiclet teeth and a bit of pink tongue poking out, making her feel she was being spun round and round on the swings again.

One evening he showed up at the store. He took Vera by the hand and demanded she show him every bolt. The manager, Mrs. Borthwick, kept looking at them with this, "What in the name of all things righteous?" look. Jaime pretended he was buying. What could he possibly be making with all this different fabric: drapery material, canvas for awnings, a white sheer meant to veil a bride? Customers were lined up, some leaving in frustration without having been served. Mrs. B. said, "May I be of assistance, sir?" so many times that Vera and Jaime screamed in unison as soon as the woman began to open her mouth. Who was this extra-terrestrially pretty boy who looked better in his duds than did most runway stick figures? Who seemed to know fabric as if he'd worked with it all his life, knew instinctively how a given length would lie across a shoulder, drape down the spine, lift in the breeze, lift with the ribcage the way a sigh will before settling? He made her feel as close to him, as intimately collusive, as a twin. While they roamed the aisles, hands diving, skimming, pulling material to the surface of deep bins, unrolling, shooting, caressing, he told her his story: where he came from (Dominica), what he loved (swimming and movies), what he wanted to be (a singer), and what he hated (hypocrisy, neediness, poverty). Finally he gathered together tens of yards of brightly-coloured stuff, promising Vera that he would be in touch, and left without paying.

She didn't see him at school all week. She sat in Spanish class pretending she was conversing with him in his native tongue. In science she stared out the window at the municipal pool across the street, and wondered if he swam with the school team, which practised there. How sleek and pretty and good he was, like an otter, so different from the boys who were forever dogging her and towards whom she presented a chilly distance. They thought she was conceited, when all she wanted was that giddy time with Jaime Alessandro again.

A week to the day they had skipped and boogied and tumbled hilariously in her workplace, he showed up at the store again. He was so changed she didn't recognize him. He wore heavy makeup, his lips outlined in black and glossed the colour of a bruise, his eyes so ringed with kohl that at first she thought he was a woman who had been beaten. But then there it was, the smile, those dazzling teeth, the imp's mad worm of a tongue.

"I'm making you something," he said. "It's not finished yet." He refused to tell her until she agreed to go to the prom with him.

She said yes. She had already said yes to another boy, but decided on the spot to renege.

"It's a dress, so don't go out and buy one." She already had, but didn't tell him that either.

"Good, then," he said. "I just wanted to make sure. I'll call you tomorrow."

He didn't call. Though she passed him in the halls, he was always distracted. "Tonight, I promise. I'm sorry. I've been so busy."

The day before the prom he called her to say that *Breakfast at Tiffany's* was playing on TV at midnight. Did she want to watch it? It was a school night, but everybody was going to cut class the next day to get ready. "I'll be right over," he said, but before she could protest, he had hung up.

She was on edge all evening waiting for him, trying to think what she would say to her parents when he showed. At eleven they kissed the top of her head. "Not too late, Vera. Big day tomorrow."

She waited on the porch so that she could intercept him before he rang the bell. At one o'clock a car stopped on the street in front of the house, let Jaime out, and sped away, squealing its tires in salute.

"Shhh!" he said, sputtering, finger to his lips. He giggled. His shirt was untucked, his hair mussed. He swayed on his way up the walk as he took deliberate, exaggerated steps.

"You can't come in. It's too late."

"Please? Oh, please, Vera Lynn?" He looked at the spot on his wrist where a watch might once have resided. "I don't think we've missed it. My favourite scene."

She told him to sit beside her. "Do you want coffee?"

"No. Don't go. Sit with me. I've been bad."

"Are you cold?" He nodded. "Stand up for a sec." She lifted the seat of the bench and took out a car blanket. Seated again she draped it around him. He moved closer and put his head on her shoulder.

"Holly gets the telegram, you see, from back home, about her brother, and she's supposed to marry the South American, and George Peppard has to duck when she throws the … it's the saddest thing."

"What is?" But he was already asleep.

Once in the night he started upright with a shout, but didn't fully wake. She pulled the blanket up from where it had fallen and covered both of them with it. When she woke again it was light and birds were chirping the news that Jaime had flown away.

"WHAT SAY YOU and me fly away together somewhere Clothes Optional and plant some little flags of our own? I was thinking Aruba. You have beautiful fingers. Nice frock, by the way. Pretty in pink."

She'd put Jaime's dress on in the bathroom and hadn't had time to change out of it before the anchorman had arrived for his appointment.

"Holding very still, please," said the doctor. Vera caught his eye above the mask and saw thunderheads gathering there. Memviziri aimed his spring-loaded gun at the spot Vera had just clipped and shaved, and he fired.

"Ow! Fuck a duck!"

"So sorry." The doctor pulled the muzzle away from the back of the man's head. He adjusted the tension, removed the tiny circle of skin and handed it to Vera. When he fired again, the impact was muted.

"Run it by me again why it is we're doing it this way?"

"You have tight skin. Some men have nice roll of looseness in posterior of their heads at neck juncture. We find the narrow strip method, which we instigated with you last time, isn't quite the perfection we are hoping to. Circle graft will be auxiliary."

"It'll even out the growth for you, give you that plush lawn look," said Vera. "Your incision is almost healed back here, by the way."

Donnelley was beginning to tell her about another operation he'd had, one she'd be particularly interested in, when the doctor cut three more plugs in quick succession, stitching the incisions closed as he went. Vera applied antiseptic and, later, a gauze bandage. Swiftly the doctor made holes the same size as the plugs along the man's hairline, where sparse and tentative fuzz was rooting, and filled them. The brusqueness of his technique was enough to silence the patient for the rest of the session.

"I thought we were going to ask him to be our spokesman," said Vera after he'd left.

"That is not spokesman. In Egypt, he who speaks this way to a woman is losing very completely and swiftly his tongue!"

"Oh, doctor, I've been hearing that kind of trash talk from men since I was thirteen years old. It doesn't register anymore. Truly. Believe me."

"That is superfluous to the matter. He will never be representational. Not of this constabulary."

This was new. She had never seen him this way. She liked it. It gave another dimension, something hard and jangly to his character, like a set of spurs.

"Do you like dinner theatre, by any chance?" she said.

"I like to dine and I like theatricals. I have not experienced the consummation of the two in my history."

"Then you're in for a treat, doctor."

JAIME WAS SPEAKING too quickly for her to catch everything, but the gist was that New York had been amazing, impossible, soul searing, exhausting and character strengthening. She shifted the phone to the other ear, found a lull and tucked in.

"I waited for you to call. I stood outside my house. The boy I had turned down—you remember, the one I'd said yes to then no—came by in his car. He told me to get dressed and he would take me, no hard feelings. He said don't worry about it, these things happen. I told him to go away and leave me alone. You were coming. I didn't want him there when you arrived."

"Yes, these things happen. What can we do? The thing is, Vera love, I didn't belong there. I could have made it, I know that in my heart, but to what end, I ask you? For the desiccation and eventual excision of my heart?"

Your heart?!

"The last thing I wanted to happen was to wake up one morning popping uppers to Vivaldi like Roy Scheider's Bob Fosse in *All that Jazz*.

Just to be able to face the day and not disintegrate? I don't think so. But tell me, didn't you always want to be Ann Reinking?"

"Oh, always."

"You're really coming to the show?"

"I said I would, Jaime."

FLOATING CANDLES IN snifters of coloured water at each table cast the only light in Folly Go Nightly. Dinner dishes had been cleared. The faces around Vera were rosy in the light. The doctor shifted his seat around to her left so that he would be able to see the performance. Angelique, Anthony and Barbara were seated closer to the stage. Seeing them together gave Vera a small pang, but it was not enough to make her want to return to Hair Apparent. As she scanned the room, she felt the doctor's hand brush and then hold hers. Their waiter, made up to be Gloria from *All in the Family*, brought them crème brûlée and coffee. Serving another table was Emma Peele, black cat-suited. And over there, that *Charlie's Angel*, that Lucy Liu—wasn't that the boy from her math class, the one with the hundred-percent average who went to Waterloo on full scholarship? She wondered if he'd perform a mock kick to someone's head, for the stir it would cause and to showcase his legs.

She was bringing her gaze back to the stage when she saw Sally Emberley at a table on the other side of the room. She was wearing a black strapless dress that complemented the Sharon Stone wig. In contrast, the man beside her looked grim. Sally beamed, leaning close to him when she spoke, aroused as if fresh from tousled sheets. He was making a brave effort, uncomfortable though evidently he was. Nothing was going to defeat her, not tonight. Vera saw him stealing glances at platinum Sally. He was unsure about his wife's motives, about this transgendered place, about his role. *Relax*, Vera wanted to say. *Stop looking for something that isn't there. It'll grow back or maybe it won't. She wants this night to be perfect, so don't ruin it.*

The numbers were all they were supposed to be: Judy in her hobo getup sitting on the edge of the stage; Marilyn breathy about diamonds; Liza wanting money, money money; Shirley urging the big spender. With each act the applause grew in strength. Sally Emberley hooted and whistled, giving everyone a standing ovation. Vera even saw her pinch Mrs. Peele's pert bum. On and on it went, the glamour expanding, spilling out over the tables, dousing their inhibitions, making them feel randy and raunchy and incognito. So that by the time Jaime hit his mark and was captive in the bell jar of the spot, and the versatile little band of musicians got its second wind and the flickering light brazed the swirling cognac, Vera had almost completely forgiven him. He was the prisoner, Brent Carver's character in *Kiss of the Spider Woman*, wretched and gloriously deluded. Perfection, she thought, turning to the doctor, squeezing his hand and smiling. As close as one could get without the seams showing.

DOCTOR MEM

△

My sister Vera cut and styled at Hair Apparent for seven years through three changes in ownership and under four increasingly tyrannical bosses until the place became too toxic for her to stay, and I'm referring not only to the bleaches, dyes and holding compounds. If she could, she'd tell you she needed a change, that she was becoming stale doing the same thing to the same sparse grey hair every day, and that if she didn't get away from Anthony, her chair neighbour, she was going to either drown him in a vat of styling gel or slit her wrists. Anthony, a talented but erratic stylist, had some kind of substance-abuse problem—Vera never elaborated—and left the salon a few months after she did. Disappeared for a stretch. I never minded him. For a while there he reproduced my boring, side-part, above-the-ears, truncated-sideburn cut every six weeks, regaling me with the more salacious gossip colouring the salon. I've never had that ten-foot-pole reaction to him that my wife and daughters do. I still see him around town. He's opened up his own hair-cutting shop where a computer store used to be. When he heard about Vera he offered condolences, some would say effusively, but that's just Anthony. He liked my sister very much, he said, and admired her skill. More than that, he said, holding onto my forearm lest I leave him before getting the golden kernel of his point, "She was good with people." His point was that she was and he wasn't. If he had half Vera's talent at putting people at ease, making them not only look good but believe that the image in the mirror was attractive, he'd be a success today. As it stands, from the sign in the window, he depends upon the nearby student traffic at reduced prices for his livelihood, and I bet his business is a fraction of what it needs to be for him to cover his rent.

Vera might still be working at Hair Apparent had she not come in early one Monday morning to find that Angelique had pencilled a walk-in into her nine a.m. slot. Vera liked to come in early after dropping Marcel—the best brother-in-law a guy like me could ask for—off at his office. Her routine was to get a coffee at Phil's, the restaurant next door to the salon, smoke some cigarettes, and play Solitaire before stepping into the day. She said she never cheated and I believe her. I like to think of her sitting in one of the booths beside the window. They all knew her there. She was a great one for holding names and a compendium of arcane personal facts in her head, this waitress's anniversary and that line-cook's kid's soccer schedule. She knew all the regular customers, the old dears having a tea while they waited for their prescriptions to be filled at the drugstore. She did their hair. That was her workaday world and she was a bright player in it. Whenever I hear people bad-mouth the service industry I feel like telling them to shove over while I fill them in about my sister. It was not an act with her. It carried on outside. I can still feel those careful soothing hands on the back of my neck and nobody but nobody touches me there. She did something miraculous with those fingers.

The walk-in waiting for her was a doctor from upstairs in the building. The way Vera told it, he needed a haircut about as much as she needed her face shaved. She knew him to see, knew about his 1962 Mercedes two-seater that he treated like a revered parent, parking it underground in two reserved spots, half on each. He drank espresso and was the reason why Phil bought the silver Italian monstrosity that's always making funny noises and getting clogged behind the counter. The thing about this doctor, though, what made her look twice the first time she saw him, were his shoes—black loafers with tassels—and even from across the lobby she knew how soft they must be. The shoes, the suit, the moustache—Omar Sharif was never better turned out.

It was one of those impossible April snowstorms that make you want to crawl into an open coffin—I mean give up, flush the catalogue seeds you got the other day in the mail, throw the bedding plants out the back door. Stunned denizens were stumbling in off the street, stamping the wet white uninvited stuff off their boots, and there, standing waiting for the elevator with his double-E in a paper cup in one hand and the other in the pocket of his trousers, the *Herald* folded under his arm, was this leading man. Oh yeah, she knew who he was. She used to kid Marcel, who's no Christmas dumpling, no dogface himself, that she could think of only two people who could tempt her: Michael Jackson (I never got that one, but hey, I'm not Vera) and Doctor Mem, the hair transplant specialist from upstairs.

Vera called him Doctor Mem, but only recently did I learn that his real name is Mahmoud Memviziri and that he's as qualified to call himself a medical doctor as I am. Egyptian by way of a stint in St. Kitts in which he was running a for-cash-only breast enlargement service. He would meet his patients in Miami, take their money and fly them to the island and his operating room. Actually, I think he got around U.S. law by taking the cash after they had landed. This all came out a couple of years ago on *60 Minutes* after another "doctor," the one who bought the practice from Memviziri, killed a woman with an improperly administered anaesthetic. This dupe claimed Memviziri was at fault because he was the one who had trained him, and although nobody could prove culpability by association, Morley Safer did track Doctor Mem all the way up here to Halifax. Why is it that men who look like they should own the world end up being the skunks?

The segment opened with, of all things, an old TV commercial of Memviziri's—one I'd seen late at night, at one or two in the morning, usually just before or after the girls in bikinis came on, posing in beach sand and surf, tinny instrumental music and a 1-900 number the only added effects. What can I say? Sometimes I can't sleep.

Doctor Mem's ad was what my daughters would call cheesy: him in a flesh-coloured skullcap, moustache similarly covered, sporting a Telly Savalas fedora. He looks directly into the camera and says something like, "Bald men, who loves you, baby?" The tough-guy spiel continues for a few more seconds, during which he lets you know what he can do, how effective his procedure is (99.8%), and where he can be found. Today he can't be found. If you believe Anthony, who cornered me in the express lane of Sobey's the other day, Memviziri is on the lam for tax evasion and for unlicensed medical practise.

You've probably figured out by now that Memviziri wasn't there to get a haircut that wintry Monday morning in April. Vera knew at a glance that the man had his black and silver coif attended to by a very expensive, very precise stylist, probably every week to ten days. She guessed it was someone who had the time to work on his hair the way an archaeologist approached a dig. Immaculate. The workmanship, like the quality of his footwear and suits, took her breath away. I can imagine her being seduced by the idea of working for a man who had no need of her haircutting skills.

At least four boys had asked her to her senior prom, including the steady beau of three months, the volleyball player she had just dumped. She'd rejected them all. You have to understand how beautiful my sister was. She had forty-year-old men propositioning her on the street. These boys—think of it. They've only just defeated the heartache of acne; they've summoned their last scrap of courage to pick up the phone, dial our house number, actually not hang up when she answers. And maybe she goes out with them a few times and maybe she even thinks that they're fine, potential sweethearts, but you know and I know what each one did to kill his chances, including the vice-principal of the high school and including the owner of the fabric store where she worked evenings and weekends. He let her know that the idea of her was embossed on the inside of his skull, so that when he closed his eyes at night, etc., etc. Think kiss of death. Never say "I love you" to a girl who hears the words almost as often as she hears "Have a nice day."

The one boy who didn't make this mistake, because he loved my sister the way you love your best friend, was Jaime Alessandro. He was the first openly gay person I ever knew about. Vera fell for him before she knew that boys could feel that way for other boys, showing how innocent or blind or simple or self-captivated she was at the age of sixteen. Nobody told her. I think she knew but refused to believe it about Jaime, who was from Jamaica or Bahamas and looked a lot like Harry Belafonte's daughter.

He was the one who, without taking a single measurement, sewed a prom dress that fit her as well as anything she had ever bought. And she was one picky clotheshorse, my sister. Our mother finally refused to shop with her. Vera could pick out the most expensive item on a rack by feel alone. She used to cry streams of tears in frustration until she was old enough to earn her own money to buy clothes, and still she was never satisfied. This was no selfish insatiable hunger, don't think that. The same Vera who could take a woman sick from radiation and make her feel like a star in a new wig was the girl who appreciated finery with a joyful expansive heart.

The dress was flamingo pink. She showed it to me. She didn't wear pink, hadn't since she was a child. This was a duplicate of something Audrey Hepburn had worn in a film, *Funny Face* or *Sabrina*. A light sheer scarf the same colour as the dress wrapped once around the neck, across the shoulders and down each side of the back. Jaime showed her how it was supposed to hang. And shoes—where had he found ones to match and how did he know her size? How did he know how to achieve any of this? I recall Vera saying that his mother and aunts were seamstresses, that he had grown up an only child, adored and spoiled in a household of women, and that every day he came home from school to watch television, usually an old movie: Ruby Keeler, Betty Grable, some gaudy extravaganza. He didn't know it at the time, but this was valuable homework for him, crucial study time.

Vera put the dress on and he waited for her to get off work. I can picture him leaning back against a cutting table, his hair trimmed severely short like a Roman emperor's, his face pale with makeup, an Isherwood death's head grinning at his creation, delighting in the shock waves, loving but not needing my sister, who at the age of sixteen going on immortal was someone who could have caused stupid men to go to war.

Perhaps I exaggerate. She is not here to contradict me as she surely would. All I have is the memory of these stories she told me, breathlessly, late at night on my bed or hers, in the dark or across many miles connected by a phone line. I used to think that if we tried hard enough we might have been able to communicate telepathically. I was convinced of this in grade ten after reading *The Chrysalids*, sure that Vera and I were endowed with minds as powerful as those mutant children in the book.

Jaime Alessandro, who seemed to know what it was to be a woman better than many women did themselves, took Vera by the hand, led her out of the fabric store onto the sidewalk, and flagged down a taxi. "Where are we going?" she said, the way you do when you know you're not going to get an answer until you can see it for yourself. She wanted to freeze this frame and spend as long as she wished in it. It didn't matter that I was her kid brother; Vera held nothing back. She made me privy to the most intimate details about her dates, which were usually with desperately groping, lust-struck boys. Vera was discerning enough to avoid, or refuse and refuse again, the rogues and the rakes, the never-at-rest Lotharios, the ones with their own money and pick-up lines. Instead, she would go out with some nice sweaty chump who was maybe good-looking, maybe not so handsome—it didn't seem to matter. She was more interested in what the boy thought, what he stood for, how independent he was, how much or how little he was going to let his life be changed by close proximity to her in a darkened movie theatre. The family car would be parked up behind ours in the driveway, often close enough that the bumpers were touching. Sometimes Romeo was so nervous that he didn't brake in time. Nice boy. Anxious boy. I was no different when I started to date.

Vera would watch me pace in a circle around the telephone or mope like a mourner after the loss of another chamber of my heart. "Is it about sex, Jay?" she would ask and I would lie at first, saying, "No!" or "What do you take me for?" or "You don't understand, you're a girl," but she knew exactly what was up.

"What I don't understand is your—I mean boys' in general—needing it so badly and constantly. It's more than a physical release, isn't it, for you?"

"Yes. It's more."

"The problem with men," she said, as if I weren't one, "is that they can't just be with a woman, enjoying her company. They have to always be plotting: how to find us, how to keep us, how to win us back. It's war all the time isn't it? We can be sitting in a restaurant ordering dessert after a movie and on the surface everything is pleasant and innocent and calm, but I'll look in his eyes and there he will be, distracted, thinking about his next move."

Knowing what she knew about men, and from such an early age, Vera must have sensed that nothing Memviziri ever did was random or spontaneous. He was waiting for her at Hair Apparent that snowy Monday morning because he needed an assistant, someone who knew hair and was restless enough or paid so poorly that she would be willing to change jobs. He had precise criteria: she had to be physically stunning, with a pleasant submissive nature, and be open to seduction. By him.

"I brought him over to my chair and started snipping. There was nothing to do. He was perfect."

"What did he say?"

"He said, Something is wrong? So I said, I'm sorry, sir, but there is not much I can do for you. Now that is not exactingly true, he said. Like that. Exactingly. I almost lost it on the spot."

"You mean laughing?"

"That's right. You certainly don't need a haircut, I said. Would you like a different colour? (Guess what? He didn't.) A tan? We have a light table in the next room. He looks at me like I've insulted his mother. Do I appear before you requiring a tan? No, I said. No, you sure don't. I doubted he wanted his nipples pierced, either."

"You're kidding. You didn't ask him that!"

She punched my bicep affectionately. "No, dummy, I didn't ask him that. When I took his bib off him he got out of the chair and started pulling paper money out of his wallet. You should've seen it: black calfskin you could put on a baby."

"You didn't take it."

"Of course not. I said, I can't charge you, and gave the back of his neck a whisk. He smelled good, like cocoa butter and aloe, and I got this crazy urge to touch his bare chest. I hoped he had hair there, some, not too much. And isn't there this oyster-shell chronometer peeking out from under his French cuff! I must pay you for your time, he says, and presses a wad of twenties into my hand. No, I tell him, I can't. Surely, he says. Something.

"Vera, I say, waiting, watching to see if he gets it. No, Mahmoud. Come back when you get shaggy, Mamood, I say. Mahmoud, he says again. It has sounds I know I'll never get my mouth around, so I say, How about

Moe? He goes, I never get shaggy. I mean, shit, I knew that was true the first second I saw him. Then he says—get this: Allow me to dine you out."

If a warning bell was sounding somewhere, Vera didn't hear it. She accepted. He told her where he worked and she said she knew that already. "Oh, so you have been surveying me!" he said, when what he meant was, "I've been watching you." The branch was salted and limed and she had made a perfect landing, not a feather mussed.

BALD MEN, WHO loves you, baby? Jesus loves you. Mummy loves you. My brother-in-law Marcel is pretty close to bald, was already doing the hopeless comb-over when he met Vera, and she thought, Here is a bald man who thinks nobody can see, and the idea squeezed her heart. Marcel came into her life well before Memviziri did and he remained the constant good husband throughout. Unlike the scrupulous and meticulous tax man he is, Marcel failed to detect anything untoward about the so-called doctor. Nor did I, for that matter. I kept going to Hair Apparent and would drop in on Vera upstairs in the hair-replacement clinic, if she was working a Saturday or a weekday evening, which she sometimes did. In the first few months working for Memviziri she was happier than I'd seen her in a long time. In her new workplace there was no gossip, no back pain or sore arches, no jealous disputes over tips and the share of the weekly earnings. No Anthony to endure.

Anthony can be one snippy fellow, I think he'd be the first to agree, but nobody, not even Vera, gave me a better cut than he did. Still, out of loyalty to Vera, I continue to patronize Hair Apparent. Saturdays I come in, sit, leaf through a *Vogue* back to front, never resting my eyes for too long on any one page, and I take whoever's free. Or they take me. I should really make appointments. I don't know, maybe I keep returning in the hope that I'll feel something of her spirit again, there where she made so many people look good. Once, I was leaving, reaching for my jacket hanging in the salon's coat rack, and my hand brushed against a soft sweater, yellow mohair, on a padded pink hanger, and I was sure it was one Vera used to wear. It was then a little more than a year since the fire at the Folly and three since she had last worked at the salon. Would they have left her sweater hanging there all that time without anyone putting it aside or claiming it? I kept my hand there. I was in view of everyone sitting in the waiting area, including the receptionist. I stepped closer, brought my face up against the garment, breathed in what I was certain was her scent. But what would I do with the sweater if I brought it home? Give it to my wife? One of my daughters? Here, honey, this was Vera's. I want you to have it. What kind of screwy karma do you catch when you wear a dead person's clothes? It probably wasn't even hers anyway.

After she began working for Memviziri, his waiting room filled with two kinds of patients. Customers is the better word. One was the candidate for hair plugs, the transplant procedure Memviziri claimed to have perfected. These were men who, because of inherited traits, were losing their hair in a wide swath off the top of the head straight back from the forehead. The other group, smaller in number, were women wanting a natural-looking wig. Often they were receiving cancer treatments and wanted something as close in appearance to their old hair as they could get. If they were really thinking ahead, they came to the clinic well before the chemotherapy began, and Vera would take photographs of their hair from all angles, sides, back and top. Then she cut the hair off. It was usually long, thick, luxuriant, lustrous; women with short, limp, colourless hair didn't care to conserve it.

After removing the hair, Vera would find as close a matching wig as possible, so that the woman could wear something suitable in the interim. What remained on her head would be very short. Vera would fit the temporary wig, comb it out, trim it to specifications, preferences, and they would leave. Whatever Doctor Mem paid Vera to do this work could not possibly have been enough.

The women returned two weeks later now used to their synthetic hair, complaining mildly about how hot the wigs could be in summer, but embracing the prop as a necessary appendage. Chemo might have commenced by then. They might even have finished a preliminary round and were looking forward to two weeks or so of rest. Vera would bring out her creation constructed of long threads of their former selves, arrange it on their heads, and with the help of the pictures make it look the way it had before everything in their lives had frozen in an inward-leaning posture straining toward treachery, invasion, betrayal, truncation. Invariably they cried, took one look in the mirror and broke into shards.

Even with Vera's facsimile of their hair now on their heads they would never quite look the way they did that first day they came in. Their skin would look different: pallid, dry, thin. They would have lost weight, not as much as they would eventually drop but enough to be noticeable. What Vera noticed more than the altered skin, melted fat, waning muscle, and thinning bone mass was the change in their eyes, which said, "She has been taking poison. A war is waging inside. Look at us: a pair of hazy, smeared panes of flat glass. Did you think a mere arrangement of dead tissue, these protein strands, was going to change anything?" One woman said, "I thought it would transform me. I thought I would be my old self again." Another said, "I didn't know how bad I looked until I put it on." Another, sobbing angrily, tore the new wig from her head, threw it at Vera, put the brassy synthetic one back on and, not stopping to right it, walked with it all askew toward the door. Before opening it to leave and without turning to look at Vera, she said, "I'll make do with this. It's really all I deserve, when you think about it."

During these exchanges Vera would be alone. Memviziri hid in his office and let his talented new assistant brave the emotional storm. "The moment I saw you," he said, "I knew you were the one I was looking for." She never called him the coward that he was. That was Vera. In her eyes she was fulfilling one unique responsibility of the job, one she had to carry out alone. She never stopped being grateful to the snake.

Vera told me that Jaime Alessandro, as he handed her into the taxi, said the same thing Memviziri had. I think Jaime meant that the moment he saw her he knew she was the one he had waited for his whole life, to play with, dress up like a doll, giggle with like sisters. He directed the driver to a club that had opened recently downtown. It was called Folly Go Nightly and it occupied an abandoned theatre beside a bathhouse that was regularly being raided by the police. The nightclub was a virtual extension of the baths, the clientele of the latter creating the audience of the former. Jaime led Vera to a tiny round table at the front near the stage and told the waiter, who like all the servers was dressed in drag, to take care of her. He brought her a big flamboyant drink in a coconut shell. It had a little parasol and bits of fruit floating in it.

"As I sat there, I felt like I was drinking something that could change my life. What was that stuff the Greeks drank?"

"Ouzo?"

"No, the gods."

"Ambrosia?"

"Right, ambrosia. I looked around and I thought, People can be who they are here, even more than they are, by dressing up like somebody else. There, the only thing men needed from me was my applause. It was like, to be male was to be elusive like a dust devil or the tip of a tongue on the back of your neck. I sat there drinking my silly show-drink, waiting for Jaime and his friends to don their costumes. All around me the tables were filling with handsome, well-dressed men. It was amazing, Jay, real gold flashing off their wrists and in the necks of their open shirts. They looked as comfortable there as they might have been in a boardroom or on a tennis court. You know the type. Picture Uncle Eldon, only younger. He knows which fork to use and when, knows how to hand his lover every desire on a glistening tray. I'm sitting there, gapped out, daydreaming about getting in and out of limousines with a man like that. We're standing at the mezzanine bar while he buys us two over-priced flutes of champagne and talks about the barely audible catch in the tenor's voice, blaming the dry air and the singer's insane schedule. It was like I was floating on the fumes of my nutty drink, loving being watched as the house lights dimmed, even if the guys checking me out preferred their own company to mine. I didn't give a hoot. I was flying.

"I was quiet in the cab on the way home. I didn't want the bubble of the evening to pop. When Jaime asked me what I thought of his performance I said that I liked it. He said, When my little sister gives a piano recital I say I liked it even if I didn't. You don't have a sister, I said. You know what I mean.

"I didn't understand the significance of everything he was doing up there—I think he was supposed to be Courtney Love doing Hello Dolly, but I told him I appreciated the quality of the performance. You got such a loud response, I told him. They were so enthusiastic. Actually, people were clapping so hard it scared the shit out of me."

"How do you mean?"

"Like he was their saviour or something. Like the only way things were going to get any better in the world was if he died."

"That's heavy."

"You're telling me. Anyway, then he says, I don't care what they thought, I want to know what you thought. So I tell him the truth. I say it left me feeling empty."

It was four a.m. and we'd been talking for an hour in low voices, so as not to disturb our parents. "I wish I'd said something like, instead of making me feel empty, his performance washed away all the crap of everyday living from my mind and replaced it with starlight and moonlight and that glowing green light in the sea. That was how I really felt. What's that word? For the green light?"

"Phosphorescence."

She wanted to phone him that instant to tell him so, to use the word. She may not have been well educated, but she cared a lot about words and meaning. She was upset because she didn't have his number and didn't know where he lived. It was too late. His mother and aunts and girl cousins were asleep. Might they have waited up for him? Did they even know where he'd been all night, what he'd been doing? Perhaps they would not have understood the reason why he, their only little man, chose to transform himself into a woman on the stage.

ONE OF MEMVIZIRI's clients was a man who read the local news on television. He was a good candidate for surgical hair replacement because his follicles grew close together and the hair at the back near his neck was thick. He had a wide roll of fat just above his shirt collar there that Vera could turn into healthy plugs. First she shaved the area. Then Memviziri began by giving the patient a local anaesthetic before slicing a strip about six inches long and an inch wide. This he handed to Vera while he sewed the incision closed. In the case of the newscaster and similarly hefty men, the effect was much like a facelift. They noticed that their collars fit better afterwards. Some even breathed easier. Because the incision was made across a thick band of hair, it healed without the scar being seen. I started watching the news at 5:30 after Vera told me. Sure enough, week by week his forehead began to shrink, the former widow's peak reaching out, it seemed, to join his eyebrows. I wish I'd taped it so that I could watch it happen in fast motion.

Vera's job was to take the band of skin, fat, and hair, and to slice it into tiny segments, each containing a healthily rooted hair or two. These Memviziri planted in incisions just wide enough to accommodate the plug. One effect of this epidermal sowing was that blood flow to the excavated area increased, new capillaries spreading like rivulets in a spring melt to nourish the seedlings. So rarely did anything go wrong that Memviziri dispensed with malpractice insurance. Recent history suggests that his best insurance was a packed bag, a false passport, and an open airline ticket to some sunny island far away.

The big-turtle-in-a-little-pond anchorman was coming in weekly for new plugs—Memviziri could plant only a few at a time, having to wait for the last incisions to heal before introducing new little saplings—and Jaime Alessandro returned after an unsuccessful attempt at achieving stardom (or anythingdom) in New York. Vera hadn't seen him for almost five years. Folly Go Nightly had reopened under new management. The bathhouse was now an upscale health club with Nautilus machines, personal trainers, whirlpools and a juice bar, but the clientele was the same.

Jaime dropped by on a day when the newsreader was receiving his last cornrow and was being obnoxiously attentive to Vera as she assisted Doctor Mem in the procedure. The lush new growth must have given the man a testosterone boost, because he directed his comments and queries to Vera in a way that made her blush, more for his lack of tact and embarrassing choice of clichéd double entendres than for the risqué references themselves. Jaime was sitting out in the waiting room common to a group of medical practitioners on that floor.

"I could see the doctor wasn't happy with the guy coming on to me like that. What I didn't realize until later was how much he'd fallen for me. He's normally so courteous with patients, a little distant but making them feel like they're the Pope or something, except without all the fawning. You know? But with this dude, I'm telling you, he stopped just short of throwing him out of the office.

"I tried to put him at ease by saying that I'd been getting this kind of thing from men all my life and that it bothered me less than a hangnail or a paper cut. But before I can finish what I'm saying, he places his hand on the small of my back and he draws me in and doesn't he kiss me? I swear, Jay, for the first time since Marcel, and maybe for the first time, period, a man kissed me in such a way that I had to grab onto the edge of the examination table to stop myself keeling over. He held onto me until I could stand on my own again. We kept looking at each other close up. I was going cross-eyed. I was thinking, Oh, this is not smart, not a prudent thing in the least. I couldn't get my arms to push away or do anything but hang on to him."

The receptionist, a pleasant and tactful person, knocked before pushing open the door to tell them that Jaime was waiting to see Vera and wasn't the buzzer on the intercom working? Memviziri let go of Vera and retreated into his office. Vera continued to stand in one spot, unsure if her legs still worked well enough to let her take a step. The receptionist gave Vera a smile and a wink.

The hair stylist at the Folly had just quit and Jaime wanted Vera to apply for the position. "No makeup, strictly hair." The cast numbered twelve and included two acrobats, a comedian and a magician. Jaime was of the opinion that they would benefit greatly from her professional expertise. "I've seen what those hands can do," he said.

"I tried to recall Jaime ever seeing me work, but all I could remember was the time I cut his hair for him back in high school. It was before he started performing at the club the first time, before he went away. It was almost graduation day and Jaime was in a right royal funk. He had no idea what he was going to do with his life. Going back to school was not an option. He said he'd rather join a monastery than do that. He said, in this voice like death, Give me a businessman's cut, Vera, so I can get an office job. The way he said businessman's cut, he might as well have been saying, decapitation."

VERA TOOK THE job at the Folly Go Nightly, cutting back her hours with Memviziri, much to his displeasure. After his display of passion she needed time away, and so came to work at the clinic all day Monday and Tuesday, but mornings only on Wednesday, Thursday, Friday, Saturday—those days when the club presented its full revue. Though she could have kept working full-time for Doctor Mem, she needed that buffer of a few hours each day between working so closely with him and entering the netherworld of the nightclub.

"Please understand, I said to him. I was straddling him. We were face-to-face in his padded swivel chair." Sometimes she told me more than I needed to know.

"You don't want to be near me, he said. I think what we're doing right now contradicts that, I said. I love you. I love Marcel. I love Jaime in a completely other way. We—this isn't going to last. I have to have the time to—if I don't take it, I'll disappear. Do you understand what I'm trying to say? No, I do not, he said. I'll disappear into you, I said. I'll lose myself. Let us go away together, he said. Come away with me. I know of an island."

He had to catch himself there, I imagine, remembering that the portal to that particular paradise was closed to him. No, she said. They would have this for as long as it lasted. She wasn't going to budge. She came to him and continued to do so during the lulls between appointments, but never in the after-hours. She told him she wasn't going to do anything to compromise her marriage.

Memviziri, having never met Marcel, maintained a courtly silence on the subject of the husband. He must have seen himself to be a kind of quixotic knight for whom honour carried the same weight as his arrogant sense of noblesse oblige. His favourite rant was that they, whoever they were—patients demanding refunds or court-enforced restitution for surgical slips, tax assessors, creditors, grim associates—did not appreciate what he did for them. They did not properly acknowledge their debt to his genius. And yet a husband, cuckold or no, stood well apart in his estimation from this gang of thieves. A husband was a nobleman in this land of unmoored appetite and domestic disintegration. He promised he would do all in his power to ensure that Marcel never learn about Vera's infidelity.

He did not release Vera, however, even those few hours a week, without telling her how much he disliked her friend, "the female impersonator." The hair specialist was no rube. He had travelled widely, had seen similar performances in Europe and Southeast Asia, and accepted with the worldly man's capacious heart all that a cosmopolitan existence might offer. The difference was that Memviziri had committed the crime of confessing not only his romantic love but his need for Vera, and as such had become that most dangerous of humans, the jealous man. He saw how much Vera loved Jaime, how her eyes grew large watching him sing and strut and prance, how they finished each other's sentences when they drank together after the performances. We made a tight little gang for a while there, for the first few weeks that the club was operating: Marcel, accepting that the only time and place he was going to see Vera during the week was then and there, where the performers made irreverent fun of the very way of life he and she led out in the suburbs; I, out of curiosity, wanting to share something with a sister who was growing not so much distant as hazy; and Memviziri, who was becoming careless in love. If he'd had a wife, his marriage would have been ruined by now. If his business had depended upon discretion, he would have had to close shop earlier than he did. As I said, for all his faults the man was empathetic, leading me to wonder whether or not he had once been married and had lost his wife to another man. Marcel, in his eyes, was an unfortunate, unwitting victim.

Can anything be finer, more invigorating to one's sense of worth and well-being, than to sit in a group of dear friends and be entertained by someone universally loved? We felt it, I'm certain we all did. Faces around us were richly lit by candlelight and flushed by the heat of the room or perhaps by the sauna next door. It was the flush of good cheer in the community of those who invest all they are in the here and the now, worshippers at a temple beyond which no life is conceivable. Their catechism was a strict devotion to pleasure and, in expressing it, one chanted one's essence over the rising din, ever so sweetly, ever so urgently into the ear of the one seated next to you, that he could not but bend to your desire. "The Blessed Trinity!" I heard an audience member exclaim after a performance in which two men, one older, the other younger, both dressed as milkmaids, manipulated marionettes and sang the yodeling song from *The Sound of Music*. "The father, the son and the holy goat!"

The sniffs, raised eyebrows, penetrating stares, and sputtering cackles following this pun were the equivalent of guffaws and backslaps anywhere else. I wish Vera had been sitting with us then, to see and hear, but she was backstage, as always, helping the next performer get ready.

Because she loved the excitement of the work, the frantic preparation that had the feel of something prenuptial, she would have done it full-time and without pay had she and Marcel been able to afford it. She quickly took on much more than she had originally agreed to do: makeup, costume repair, set construction, sound checks, lighting design, snack runs—anything and everything, to be close to the hum, close to Jaime. When he fell in love with this boy or that, and when he plummeted out, she cried with him. When he threatened to leave because of an unspoken slight that only he had perceived, she convinced him to stay. When he came off the stage and the applause continued, and before he went back out for his encore, she was there to pat him back into shape, to give him a bolstering drag off her du Maurier, and help gather the light around him again.

"You're such a wife," he said to her once, meaning, "Where would I be without you, you beautiful helpmeet, you capital-f Friend?"

"You're such a wife," I said to mine after I had told her about Vera's affair with Memviziri. We were driving back from her funeral.

"What is that supposed to mean?"

"I only meant that until you find yourself in Vera's position—"

"Which I never will."

"And let me be the first to praise you in your constancy."

"Not appreciating the sarcasm."

"Who said—?"

"You used the word, 'wife' the way you use the word 'spinster' or 'fishmonger.'"

"I'm sorry. All I meant was—"

"Vera was an adult. She was in charge of her destiny. She made choices."

"I'm not condoning what she did. I'm only saying—"

"Yes, that you understand. By all means, let us understand."

"And the alternative?" I said.

"The alternative is that we act like grown-up people. The alternative is responsibility, self-control, considered behaviour."

Vera wasn't there to defend herself and I wasn't in the mood to argue. To tell the truth, I was bereft with guilt as much as mourning. I should have told Marcel what was going on. He would have been angry, he might have hit her, but she would be alive today.

I think about the three of us, Memviziri, Marcel and me, sitting in the audience, sometimes together, sometimes apart, watching Jaime and his fellow performers but adoring Vera, the incandescent thought of her, with each his own motive and intensity. Tired of late-night, second-hand accounts, I was there to be part of her world. Naïve Marcel tried to understand her, he really did. I think all he wanted was to spend whatever time he could with her. They had a grateful and understanding babysitter. Memviziri, with his ever-present demitasse at hand, would stare at Jaime, quietly seething.

When the alarm rang, I thought that it was coming from next door and that the bathhouse was being raided again. Marcel and I stood. We were sitting with two of Vera's cronies from Hair Apparent. Memviziri had disappeared. Smoke was beginning to waft out across the little stage. When the audience saw that it wasn't dry ice and part of the act, they didn't panic. In fact some looked annoyed by the inconvenience. I waited until I saw Vera and we filed out the front entrance together. It was cold out on Barrington Street, mid-January, and many of the performers had come outside wearing only their costumes. Gallant patrons took off their mohair overcoats and draped them over slender bare shoulders. The fire engine came wailing down Spring Garden from the west. Someone said, "Where's Jaime?" He said it in the Spanish way, a moan, a sigh of distress. Nobody was asking where Doctor Mem was.

Before I noticed she was gone, and before anybody could stop her, Vera had ducked under an arm and squirmed through the wall of huddled bodies. Then the firemen were there, telling everybody to move to the other side of the street. I asked where Vera was. Somebody said he saw her go back inside the club. Marcel started crossing the street, but a policeman waved him back. We told them that there were people still inside. My sister was in there. "My wife," said Marcel. Don't worry, they said, we'll get them out. Just stay put.

The building, a yellow-brick theatre with apartments above, built around the time of vaudeville, went up like the model schoolhouses we used to burn as the culmination of Victoria Day fireworks. It was majestic, almost pure flame, sun-strong and smokeless at its apogee. The heat drove us up the street to where it meets Spring Garden Road. We watched the water freeze on the roof and on the sides of the Folly. Firemen on the ground worked in pairs to control the hoses. They stepped this way and that with the force, and it looked like choreography. In a bucket on the end of a raised hydraulic arm, one of their fellows directed a gushing stream through a broken upper-storey window.

After the fire was extinguished, they brought Jaime and Vera out together. They were wrapped in identical grey blankets and carried by two firemen, one still angel in the arms of each. They looked to be merely asleep, and I expected the firemen to begin the routine resuscitation that usually relieves suspenseful TV dramas. When they laid their bodies out on the sidewalk and covered their faces with the blankets, I went berserk, running up to them, demanding they do something, smashing my fist into the wall.

The three upper, unused storeys of the building were charred wrecks, but on the ground floor, where the fire started, in the hallway outside the tiny dressing room where Jaime and Vera were found, fire damage was minimal. The flames spread up the inside of the walls, leaving the nightclub looking eerily intact though covered by a film of ash, the floor awash in black water. The autopsies showed that Vera died of asphyxiation from the smoke, and Jaime, from an overdose of morphine administered by hypodermic injection, the needle still in his arm.

I ask Vera, late at night when I can't sleep, "Morphine? Come on. Really? That's stuck-in-the-projects, ex-con stuff."

No answer.

"The needle was sticking out of the side of his left bicep, high up. I distinctly remember you saying that Jaime was left-handed like you."

As always she's as quiet as the Sphinx. A slight shake of the head: You know the answer, bro', figure it out.

"Left-handed. Like Doctor Mem."

She cracks the faintest Mona Lisa grin.

"I'm going to find him. Drag him back here to face justice."

She winks: Sure, O.J., you go right ahead and do that.

CITY OF MY DREAMS

CITY OF MY DREAMS

AFTER HE SAW Dot settled, Breem retraced their steps and descended a second flight to the men's room.

He entered a stall, locked the door, lifted the toilet seat and, steadying himself with his left hand braced against the cubicle's marble wall, lifted his right foot until his shoe was resting on the rim of the bowl. He plucked at the fabric at his knee, which looked like a stick was trying to poke through, and pulled the pant leg upwards. At home Dot always sat on a low stool in their bathroom and helped him empty the bag. They'd forgotten to do it before leaving the apartment. Breem bent over with tremulous hesitancy, having to straighten twice and wait for his head to clear. He tried a third time. He could reach the plastic bladder but not the end of the tubing with its little clamp. His foot slid off, luckily not into the water, and he gave up.

When he got back to his seat he fired a shot of nitroglycerin under his tongue.

"How did you do?"

"Just peachy," he said.

"We should have bought seats at a table," she said, her worry for him dressed as annoyance. "Would it have killed them to install an elevator?"

"They wanted a hundred and fifty for a seat down there. You're not saying you came to dance, are you?"

She glowered at him through slit eyes. When she reached for the handle of her cane, she knocked it off its perch on the armrest and it rattled onto the floor. The woman sitting beside her picked it up and secured it between their seats. Dot thanked her, making a gentle joke about aged reflexes.

"I won't argue with you about the elevator," said Breem.

"Hush now," she said, "it's starting."

Hired waltzers were emerging, a pair of pairs, one from each wing below the stage, the women looking girlish but brittle in their full, monochromatic, metallic looking skirts. They were taller than their partners, bank-clerk milquetoast, all except for one dashing Aga Khan and his China-doll partner, a couple so smooth that Breem had to look to be sure that their feet were actually moving. A few seats away from where they were sitting, in the balcony that faced the stage, a young man snagged each pair of dancers in a brief spotlight.

A small man with a large voice came onto the stage to sing "I'm In Love With Vienna" in the style of Richard Tauber. After the applause he said that his career had begun here on this stage when he was a music student at this university. "How long ago was that?" he said, ruminating theatrically. "Twenty-two years? Impossible!"

Breem's hernia was older than that.

"Did I mention?" the tenor continued, mentioning Isaac Stern, Andrew Lloyd Webber, Beverly Sills, Maureen Forrester. "Bear with me. If I can have but a few more words."

"If you had fewer words you'd be a better public speaker."

"What's that, Gene?"

With an unsurprising flourish the singer brought his *apologia pro vita sua* full circle to return his audience, after a tour of the world's great concert halls, to the present humble stage, which, he assured them, was no less important than the Royal Albert or Carnegie Hall, for here fledgling talent first took wing.

"Who are we clapping for now?" Her hearing was selective.

"The queen," he said archly.

The dapper *voxmeister*, alumnus extraordinaire, homecoming hero, continued. "The appeal, yes, there I go, I've said it now: money. The reason I'm here."

No, thought Breem, the reason you are here, little sir, is that your mum and your dad…

"... able to take the time? Well, I can tell you truthfully, I didn't have to think about it. We make time for urgent requests such as this, we push everything else aside. The schedule can be altered. Berlin can wait."

"What's the money for, did he say?"

"Grand pianos," said Breem. "Unlike us, they don't improve with age. The wood dries out." Noah built the Ark of gopherwood. After forty days damp, millennia on Ararat to bake and freeze. There was a stress test for you.

"And so, to all and sundry, my sincere thanks. All thanks to you," he said, gesturing to the tables with a sweep of open arms. "And let us give thanks for the gift of music."

Another grandee took the stage: chairman of the music department. "A new Yamaha, ladies and gentlemen, even with our academic discount..."

"Is it a real discount or only academic?" said Dot.

"... twenty-two thousand and change."

"I can buy a new car for less," said a man sitting behind them.

"That's the unit cost," the speaker continued, "and we require—oh, let's pick a number, shall we?" And the number shall be five.

He indicated with word and gesture an angel seated at a table close to the stage, and directed the spot to shine there, just left of center. Stand up, Mrs. Angel. Now, everyone, a big smacking of clappety-clap, for she has been so very generous. Ten-K simoleons has she granted us, yes, toward a new grand pianoforte, and, get this, another ten toward the cost of "freeing up" world-class chamber musicians to come to our fair town. "Did you know, for example, that a cellist must pay for two airplane seats?"

Breem pictured musicians released from captivity and brought here in leg irons to perform. As a boy he'd seen shackled Russian bears banging on steel drums in time to music played by a brass band. Another time the animals skated on ice.

He drifted, blades biting, planing. Lily Lake, Saint John, New Brunswick, frigid night air, white brilliance under electric lights strung tree-to-tree. Romance in every exhaled plume. Fur-clad musicians playing Waldteufel and Strauss. *An der schönen blauen Donau.* His conditioned response when he heard it now or simply thought about the melodies. He and Dot hadn't lived in Saint John for sixty years and yet nowhere else was home. Home was a smooth, cleared, frozen lake. No comfort aside from sleep and bladder relief matched that music, that silvered memory. In that timeless place he had tireless legs, the lungs of an athlete.

There were more girls than boys in the production, he noticed, assuming that this was a command performance. Three times as many, he guessed. What were they doing studying music here? The university was known for economics, business, medicine, engineering. The speaker wouldn't say. Had Breem been a rich man and hadn't had to worry about keeping enough money aside for catastrophic care, he might have given a large sum toward an entrance scholarship for a deserving baritone who played hockey. The young men now on stage were engaged in a comic tribute to womanhood. Look at them. Someone once praised their adenoidal voices and this is the consequence. In a can-can line they were loud and harmonic, eliciting easy laughter.

One doughboy strode forward to be paired with a debutante who, in Breem's judgment, outshone the lad the way a halogen headlight drowns a firefly. *O Deus ex machina*, save him, this greasy-locked, adipose croaker who has become—look now—distracted by a music stand that is lowering untouched. Did we mention money for new music-stands, folks? Breem could almost hear the accompanying descent, through at least an octave, of a child's party-favour whistle.

It's your line, the deb mimed. The dufus caught up. There you go, Charlie, thought Breem, you're back where you began. Almost a strange loop. That's the joy of lieder. Except that you missed an entire. She's all done and you still have. What do they call you at home, Off-Key Kavanagh? Merciful Mahatma, you just had to snuggle up real close didn't you? And didn't the clod take hold of her two, slender, patrician hands in his chubby lunch hooks and—hey, that was smooth. Was he seeing this correctly? The boy had worked his lardipose bulk around behind her and wrapped his arms around front. She was fair, as they used to say to encapsulate immodest beauty in a modest word, and svelte, but with hard, unforgiving curves. Like a head-bobbing baby, any man lulled in love with her could come away bruised on such a collar bone. It made Breem feel kindlier toward the untalented lunk. She was clearly the type to keep promising a turn around the ice, though whenever you saw her she was with a different bloke.

"Did we what?"

"Dance cards," he said. "Up at Lily Lake, when we'd skate."

"More than possible."

Breem heard, Third of a dance. You-who, who'll bid me a third of a dance? Anyone? She was, this same ice princess in the sweaty clutches of a bumpkin, someone Breem had sat behind in high school, three grades in a row because their last names began with the same letter, and she appreciated it, she told him one day after graduation but before he headed overseas. She was going out to British Columbia to work in a resort hotel. Just have to, can't hardly wait to get away! She liked knowing that he sat behind her, because she knew he was the type never to play tricks on a girl. It was like I forgot you were even there, she said. It was a real comfort, Eugene, thank you. Be careful in the war.

Was Blondie cringing to have Oily Toad holding her so close? Was that honking supposed to be musical? You're supposed to goose her, not be one! A love duet straight out of *Duck Soup*. He knew what the hopeless boy was thinking: must try, must be a trouper. Meanwhile, the orchestra leader had regained his perch. Now were they finally going to hear some Strauss? *Bitte?*

Maestro was getting into it. Breem might have said that the man was getting down, except that he was bouncing on his toes. Eye-poking baton, ponytail cascading down the back of his tuxedo jacket, white hightop basketball sneakers. He looked to Breem to be trying to gain enough height to catch the woodwinds at mischief in the back row. Breem had to hand it to the man, he was getting a big sound out of those kids. Introducing the next number, the band leader mumbled and had to be corrected as to the order of performance. Dynamic Duo: Shrimp Hipster, conducting like a cheerleader, and the mc, Wireless Mike roaming the dance floor, the pair tag-teaming, a couple of toffs in tuxes. Similarly garbed swells and their dates had shelled out to masticate prime rib, quaff vintage plonk, sip *café au lait*, lick chocolate mousse off their dewy upper lips while the Breems and the other plebs peered down upon them like beneficent gargoyles.

Announcement: Everyone up and dance. Space down there between the tables. No rug to cut or shirr. Some did, could, laughably. No derision allowed. Bravo, thought Breem, you brave sophomore standing up with the prettiest lass. The undergrad covered his gracelessness with a jittery side-to-side bounce, she too gracious not to follow his lead. The boy pumped her arm up and down as if he were working a handle. Laughter lit their faces. Only the young can be ridiculous and remain beautiful.

Breem looked up and across the nothing air to the gallery perpendicular to the one he and his wife occupied. Dot was snoring lightly, a bumblebee. A young woman, tall, brunette, returned his gaze. Not one of his daughters or granddaughters looked like this. The ancient Greeks, Michelangelo, Rodin took pains to remove the rubble hiding such ideal forms. She wore a long gown, new-skin pink, with a fitted bodice of a lighter shade. Breem squinted, decided cream. He hadn't seen that particular colour since home-delivered milk in glass pint bottles. Her legs were so long that she had to sit on the diagonal at the end of a row, her feet in the aisle formed by shipboard-steep steps. Her chin rested on her hand in an elbow-on-knee posture of contemplative boredom that could also have been constrained rapture.

A porcine type sat next to her. She looked upon the waltzers lovingly. Was she dreaming of escape, of joining the princely ball, tripping lightly down a marble staircase, throwing a shoe as the narrative demanded?

In the intermission Dotty woke.

"Only a minute or two."

She patted his arm to tell him she knew he was fibbing.

"Do you need to?"

"No," he said, not wanting to repeat the ascent from the underworld. "You?"

"I'll be fine until we get home. We've been married sixty-one years, I think I can hold my water another hour."

A young man sitting two seats away from the statuesque beauty looked across at the Breems as if he had heard them. Breem had fresh eyes after recent cataract surgery, and so detected in the young man's regard something akin to salutation. The young did not naturally pay tribute to decrepit age. Breem continued to watch him after he had looked away. Was he a member of the party that included Aphrodite and her portly seatmate? It used to bother him, this not knowing. Now it was enough to be relatively pain-free, listening to Johann, Jr, the Viennese equivalent of Barry Manilow, watching limber people dance, the evening devoted to simple-minded romance, as if romance could solve anything, keep us from the grave. And yet it could, temporarily. But life passed too quickly for beauty to reside chained to a troll. What it must peel from one's spirit to capitulate so. Were she his granddaughter he would have told her that.

He looked over to see the statue rise from her seat. Her companion had her by the wrist. She wrenched free of his grasp. The music masked what they were saying to each other. She lifted the hem of her gown and climbed the short flight of stairs to the corridor that ran around three sides of the hall, almost at ceiling level. She disappeared behind a pillar. Her loud heels hammered behind the Breems, out a set of double swinging doors and down the central stairs to the lobby. If ever turmoil had been broadcast in an exit, this was the model.

They were massing on stage, all the students who had performed, their professors and the aged ballroom-dancers, to sing "*Wien, du Stadt meiner Träume.*" The words were printed on the last page of the program. Dot sang in a weak voice. *Wien, Wien, nur du allein.* It was her favourite. Usually she belted it out. Though this was the evening's culmination, Breem wanted to be elsewhere, anywhere but rooted here. Before the singing had ended, all around them rose a forest of legs in an ovation of relief. He'd had his waltz music, his schmaltz music, but for the first time it was not enough. It hadn't soothed him, had in fact put him into a palsy of agitation. The applause continued in opposition to his desire.

He leaned close enough to whisper, "Must dash, Dot. I'll be back to help you down after the rush has subsided." She looked wan.

She patted his hand where it rested on her forearm. "The letter N."

"How's that?"

"Dash-dot. N for noodle. Do you need me to...?"

"No, I'll be fine. Sit tight and keep exercising that marvelous brain of yours. You're looking a bit weary."

"I can still run circles around you, Eugene Breem. With or without a cane."

He waited for people to pass, until he had a clear path up the short flight that led from their seat row to the main staircase. Eleven steps, no railing. At the top he paused, leaned against the jamb of the double doors. He waited until he'd got his breath back and his heart rate had subsided, before moving through to the corridor. He picked the left-hand choice of two sets of stairs that joined halfway down and continued to the lobby. This time the descent was easier. His viscera felt heavy like a sack of water and he wished he'd put on his truss, though it interfered with the catheter, but there was no pain.

The lobby was filling quickly with eddies and clots of people retrieving coats and shuffling outside. Most of the heads around him were snowy white like his. Being part of a geriatric herd like this, with its lack of urgency, its good-natured inertia, usually didn't bother him. But he couldn't see the young woman and it made him feel agitated. Had she been that far ahead of him? Only a minute or two, surely. No, probably more like five. Everything happened so quickly, before he was ready, before he had a chance to appreciate it. She could be already home. Her seatmate, as far as Breem knew, had made no effort to follow her. What exactly Breem thought he could do to comfort the girl, he wasn't sure. It would be all she needed, another old man interfering in her life. What would he say to his granddaughter? Find somebody your own age. Pay attention to everything, relish every experience, because it's so soon over.

That wasn't the reason why he had chased after her. He thought Dotty would have laughed at his use of the word "chase." It wasn't to impart grizzled wisdom. Even an old, worn-out, clogged heart like his, he realized, was capable of the flutter of infatuation. Just a word, an exchanged pleasantry. He knew how to make people smile. Make this pretty girl smile through her tears, that's all he needed.

By chance, as he was being taken along toward the main door, he looked over his shoulder and caught a glimpse of her, cream and pink, above the dandelion tufts of grey and white. Breem turned and began to push upstream. "Excuse me. Sorry. Forgot my. Pardon." She was standing at the opposite door, the one that led to a parking lot. Don't go out, he thought. His and Dotty's coats were hanging closer to the main door and the late winter air sweeping into the lobby was quickly chilling him. Since reaching the bottom of the stairs he was feeling a familiar tightness in his chest. His abdominal sack was heavier, more sluggish, sending periodic jabs of pain upwards into his gut and down the inside of one leg, the one with the bladder bag strapped to it. The Velcro fastener irritated the skin there. When he'd turned his head to look behind him, he'd triggered the vertigo and now everything was mobile, the floor, the walls, as if shaken by an undulating earth-tremor.

When he reached the spot where she was standing like an usher, he could hardly see. He could make out the dividing line of her dress, just below his eye level, and heard her ask him if he was all right. She took hold of one of his arms at the bicep. It was a strong grip that eased off when she felt how little flesh was there. His vision returned slowly. She guided him toward a bench and sat beside him.

"Your colour's coming back. Is there someone I can call?"

"My wife. I've left her upstairs."

"I'll go up and get her. Where is she sitting?"

"No. I just need a minute."

She insisted and so he described the section where Dot was waiting.

"She might not go with you," he said.

"So give me something to convince her. What's your name?"

He told her.

"Okay, Gene. I'll tell her Gene's waiting in the lobby. He says...?"

"Tell her Lily Lake. Tell her Gene says remember Lily Lake."

He watched her ascend the staircase. Her Canio met her partway down. They spoke in low voices, and again Breem couldn't make out what they were saying. She crossed her arms at first then let them drop. The man made no move to touch her until they began to climb the stairs together.

The pain in his abdomen was persistent now. He'd had the catheter and bag long enough to know that it was probably full and beginning to back up into his bladder. He found his nitro in his pocket and gave himself another spray under the tongue. The stairs leading to the basement and the men's room were just there, across from where he was sitting. The urgency brought him to his feet. He waited for the light-headedness, and when it didn't come he began to walk gingerly. He got to the head of the stairs and stood looking down. Railing, dimly lit, clear, no traffic, estimated fifteen, twenty steps. Don't think about having to come back up. A long jab of pain robbed him of breath.

"How you doing, old timer?" The portly man, the goddess's unworthy escort. Who you calling old? "Need to get down there? Let me give you a hand."

"No need."

"Let me be the judge of that. Here, we'll go down together."

Where was Dotty? Where was the young woman in pink? Breem distrusted this stranger, but bowed to a higher exigency and put himself in the fellow's care. They descended, one step at a time, stopping briefly with two feet on each one. With one hand he gripped the rail, the other, the crook of the younger man's elbow.

"My wife."

"Serena's with her," said the man. "Don't worry."

At the bottom, Breem was able to walk unaided. They went into the washroom together. He had written formal examinations in this building in the early 1950s, and with pre-test jitters had tried not to think about anything except the subject at hand, his imminent trial, as he stood leaning into one of these tall ceramic basins. New chlorine cakes sat primly pungent atop rusting grates. In his memory the urinals, gleaming up-ended sarcophagi, were a longer, deeper, more imposing array.

There was no delicate way to do this. He wanted to tell this young swell that he'd played hockey in his day, in a tough mercantile league with men five and ten years his senior, and he'd held his own. Dotty wore speed skates not figure skates and nobody could catch her. When they skated together, he had to be careful of her long sharp blades. Soon enough they fell into the rhythm of the waltz and it was as if they were one four-legged animal. Sometimes a singer or a choir would provide the music. The musicians went into the heated pavilion to get warm. When Breem lost feeling in his feet it reminded him of the sensation of having skated too long in the cold. That painful tingling as feeling returned. His son used to call it ginger ale in the toes.

He explained what had to be done. They were the only two in the washroom. Breem stood near enough to a urinal that the man had only to kneel on one knee, as if proposing marriage, reach under the pant leg, find the tube, direct it toward the grate and open the flow. The bag emptied quickly, filling with what had backed up. Breem closed his eyes. It seemed to take an hour for there to be nothing left. He had nothing to say to alleviate the awkwardness.

The man clamped the tube, tucked the end back into Breem's sock, and stood. "Good as new," he said. "I'll have to get me one of those. Sure beats having to zip and unzip all the time."

"You can have it," said Breem.

"Yeah, I guess you're right about that."

Breem told him about the operation he was waiting for. It would core out his prostate to relieve pressure on the urethra. "Then I can ditch this whole get-up."

The man told him his name: Bill. It seemed like a natural point to introduce themselves. Bill had a new-car dealership outside of town. He was on his second marriage and they were crossing a patch of rough water, he and Serena. She was a fair bit younger than he was, Breem had probably noticed, and Bill had somewhat of a jealous streak. It had been his idea to take in a bit of musical culture. Serena—sometimes, Bill said, he wasn't sure he was going to be able to hold on to her.

From a distance came the sound of a siren. Ambulance, not fire, thought Breem. He knew the difference. It grew louder until it stopped close by.

"Dot is going to be wondering what happened to me."

"Mr. Breem."

"Call me Gene."

"Gene. Right. Gene, did you enjoy the music?"

"It was all right. Gives you hope to see all that talent, those bright kids."

"You can say that again. Serena wanted me to take her downstairs to dance. She got mad at me when I said I dance like a drunken bear."

"I've seen elephants dance. To Strauss, no less. They're lighter on their feet than you'd think."

"I should've made more of an effort. I don't want to take her for granted. She's such a knockout. What she's doing with a guy like me, I'll never know. Don't want to make the same mistake twice."

"Thank you for..."

"Don't mention it, Gene."

"We should get back up there."

"Gene, there's something I have to tell you, something serious."

"Then I better sit down."

Dot's favourite word was *millefleurs*, the name of her china pattern. She pronounced the French flawlessly, but said "flowers" as if referring to rivers. She'd often said that were she to return to school she would study languages. There were a few years, after the children had grown up and moved away, to schools and jobs, other provinces, other countries of the world, when she said she was going to enrol in university courses. Breem, newly retired, wanted to travel, and so Dorothy shelved her desire for higher education. He said she could learn a language better if she spent some time in the native country. All she needed was to buy some of those language tapes. But it wasn't only to become fluent that she'd wanted to go back to school; she'd wanted to read the great books, grapple with their ideas. She was the smart one, puzzling, making up her own codes. Her father, a Marconi man, taught her Morse code when she was five. She was forever tapping messages to him on the table, but he rarely got it. How were you supposed to keep track of it all, or know what was a dot and what, a dash? "What message did I just send you?" "That I'm the handsomest man in the world?" "Exactly!"

Men fell away quicker than women. Breem's heart. You must be quiet as mice, children, your father is resting while he listens to his music. We must be particularly mindful of his angina. I have an angina, one of his daughters said once. How old would she have been? Three, four? No, you don't. Yes I do, I'll show you. Her older sister took her aside to clarify and differentiate. One will severely restrict your life and may kill you. The other is a heart ailment. It became his and Dotty's favourite late-night joke. Remember what our little enchilada said? And tell me, Gene, since you men are so smart, what's the difference again?

Paramedics, a man and woman, came down the stairs. Serena was just behind them. The emergency workers walked over to where the men were sitting side-by-side on the floor outside the washroom. Serena looked grave and kept her distance. Bill got up and went over to her.

"Mr. Breem, is it?" the woman asked him.

"Yes?"

"Do you need assistance, sir?"

"Yes, I believe I do."

"Mr. Breem, we have your wife in the ambulance. We have to take her to the hospital. It's not a good situation."

"You're telling me."

"She was very poor when we got to her," said the male medic. "No vitals. A doctor still has to verify. You should come along, too."

They didn't know about Dot, about how she could sleep through the loudest disturbances at night. Sometimes he'd wake in the middle of the night and it would appear she wasn't breathing. She'd be lying there as still as a mannequin, a minute, two, and he'd be about to shake her awake when she'd take a shuddering breath, raspy, rattling, as if she'd broken the surface of the water after having been under a long time. The relief he'd feel to see her chest rise and fall.

He tried to get to his feet. His pant leg got pushed up, revealing the bag, which he knew had a few more dribbles in it. He didn't want these people seeing, and so he tried to smooth the fabric down. Too late. Bill came and began to help him up, a hand under each armpit. The female paramedic told him to wait, they'd bring the stretcher down. How silly was this? Dot was sleeping in public again and he was being manhandled by somebody he hardly knew. It was sure nuts, the way things turned out. You get up to give a young woman a few words of comfort and encouragement and what happens? The Pagliaccio she's married to follows you into the men's room with an altogether perverse sense of the limits of common decency and proceeds to make himself all too familiar.

He felt inordinately tired. It took so much effort to maintain this level of indignation. Then he remembered what Bill had done for him and what Bill's beautiful young wife, Serena, had done. He hoped that Dotty hadn't been snippy with the girl. She could be sharp-tongued when she first woke up, especially if she hadn't got enough sleep. He wasn't sure he'd buy tickets for this performance next year. Granted, there'd be a new crop of music students, and perhaps one or two would really stand out. Talent never needed an interpreter, as far as he was concerned. He'd see what shape they were in next year. He'd leave it up to Dot. She was the one with the bad hips. If she were up to it, they'd come back, see what the young people had cooked up as a fundraiser. If not, they'd stay home and he'd put on that video their son bought them, the one with the Dutch orchestra leader and the soothing arrangements.

The paramedics were there again after having gone away for a spell, he couldn't say how long, and this time they had a gurney with them. They lowered it as far as it would go and helped him up so that he could sit on the edge, swing his matchstick legs up and lie back. They fastened soft straps across his chest and thighs. Nothing new: last month alone Dot called the ambulance to come for him three times. They carried him up to the foyer, keeping his head high and the stretcher as level as possible. At the top of the stairs they lowered the wheeled legs. It felt strange not to have Dot there, the small overnight bag containing his change of clothes resting between the handles of her walker. She would say, Don't mind me, just go ahead, I can call a taxi. Nonsense, they always said, you're coming with us. She would ride up front, beside the driver, while the other paramedic would stay close to Breem, monitoring his blood pressure and heart rate. Some of the EMS workers were cheerier than others, and some, all business, were reluctant to make small talk. The newer ones let their shock and slight revulsion show on their faces. They'd toughen up. A few more weeks on the job and they'd see far worse than Breem. He felt like crowing, Look at me. I'm living proof that a man can lose everything, skin, bone mass, muscle, hair, fat, dignity, and still be alive!

This was a first: he and Dot riding the same ambulance as patients. She'd be frightened. He'd have to be sure to make her laugh. The angina joke. He would hum their favourite pieces from the concert. Who did she think had been the best singer this year? He thought he knew who he liked, but didn't always know for sure until after he'd talked it over with Dotty, who reminded him that the future stars weren't always the ones that attracted your attention on stage, at least not in this show. The talent tended to hang back. They didn't know how to promote themselves yet.

It took someone perceptive to recognize this, someone like Dot. *Nur du allein.*

"Hang tough there, Gene," said Bill as the paramedics slid Breem into the back of the ambulance. Dot lay beside him, her eyes closed, as still as moonlight on a frozen lake.

SPEEDWELL

SPEEDWELL

BEING NOW UPON the point of departing from this quarter of the World; I think no place could be more proper than this, to give some farther, and more general account of the Navigation in these seas, and on these coasts; for the more particular use of such who may have a call thither for the future, who can never receive too much instruction and advice in the most prudent methods of carrying on their Voyage, so as to answer the end of their Expedition...

> —*George Shelvocke, A voyage round the world by way of the great South Sea, perform'd in the years 1719, 20, 21, 22, in the Speedwell of London, ...London, 1726.*

I HAD BEEN READING in Shelvock's Voyages a day or two before that while doubling Cape Horn they frequently saw Albatrosses in that latitude, the largest sort of sea-fowl, some extending their wings twelve or fifteen feet. "Suppose," said I, "you represent him as having killed one of these birds on entering the South Sea, and that the tutelary Spirits of these regions take upon them to avenge the crime."

> —*William Wordsworth, Notes to "We Are Seven," 1798.*

He holds him with his glittering eye—
The Wedding Guest stood still,
And listens like a three years' child:
The Mariner hath his will.

—*Samuel Taylor Coleridge, "The Rime of the Ancient Mariner"*

It was the last time my daughters would think that spending two days in an enclosed space with their father might be an enjoyable thing to do. Burke was thirteen, Moll, nine. Their mother, Victoria, couldn't take the time away from her clothing store. Her exact words were, "You know we can't afford it." This jab at my employment status notwithstanding, the road trip with the girls had been her idea. It would give us breathing space in our troubled marriage, time to reflect. It would, we hoped, stir a fresh breeze to fill our slack sails.

The car was an eleven-year-old Chevy Cavalier without air conditioning. From Halifax we drove to Saint John and crossed the border at St. Stephen. The landscape, speed limit, type of town and quality of road changed with predictable regularity. Every ten miles or so, we came to another town. There was no circumventing them. Late in the afternoon of that first day of driving, I felt fuzzy-headed from the heat and humidity, annoyed at having to continually slow down, and benumbed to variety in both the natural and the constructed world. One town would be shockingly poor, the next, prosperous. In one, the houses looked barely able to withstand rain or a moderately stiff wind. The next would look like a municipality designed and built on an endowment: Carnegieville situated so close to its adjacent Potterstown that we could see the dividing line where the quality of the blacktop changed.

When I pointed out this economic patchwork to the girls, they began to pay attention and had soon made a game of it. Burke, poor by choice (her mother the entrepreneur wasn't there to correct her), called her side of the divided score-page, "Burke's Barrios." I gave her the word and explained its meaning. Every time we drove through a poor town, in Maine, New Hampshire and Vermont (the game fizzled before we reached

New York State), Burke got points, her score dependent upon the number of empty, broken or boarded-up windows she could count. When we came to an affluent place, Moll would count what she called mansions. "Moll's Mansions" had to be white in order to qualify (her own limitation) and they had to have at least two storeys and a front porch. She began to include all houses that fit that description until Burke explained the difference between a mansion and a regular dwelling.

"Basically," said Burke, "if you can fit Baba's house into one of these and still have room for a dance *and* a swimming pool? Indoors? That's a mansion." The new definition severely limited the number of Moll's allowable ticks on the tally sheet. The rules said that each point had to be acceptable to both.

"That's not a poor town," Moll would argue, "that's just working class."

"Working class is poor."

"No it's not. If you're working class you get a pay cheque and that's money in the bank. How can you be poor with money in the bank? Dad, tell her."

Intently watching for the first sign of a motel where we might stop for the night, I declined to get involved in the dispute. I could still hear her mother in Burke, who might well have been upbraiding me in particular: in April I had come home to announce that after seven years as a patents lawyer I was quitting and going back to school to become a history teacher.

"They are called the working poor. They work in menial jobs and barely make enough to live on. Some of them are working two jobs and all they have time for is to fall into bed at two in the morning and wake up when the cat gets them up to pee at six."

"She said pee."

"That's what Mom says. That's why you never see any of them outside. They're all working their fingers to the bone. It may look like a rich town, but appearances can be deceitful."

Moll, without a counter-argument, grew silent. Her mother in Burke's place would have swooped in for the kill at this point, calling into question her opponent's definition of prosperity. "That may look like a big house where rich people live, Moll dear, but look at all the cars parked in front. That's way too many cars for one family, even a rich family. Look closely at the vehicles themselves. See the dents, the rust spots? That, my girl, is a mansion converted into flats. If any rich people live there I'll eat my napkin." Really, Victoria should have been the lawyer.

Burke didn't have her mother's instinct for the decisive stroke, but she had something Victoria could never claim, the good sense to pull back for the sake of all. Having sat in the stifling car for ten hours, and at the end of her endurance, tolerance and imagination, the clever girl knew that without the game the desperate hour, the one without end, would descend upon us all the sooner.

I DON'T REMEMBER much about the second half of the trip. When we got into the car the next morning, we were still shaken by what had happened in the motel room the night before. Burke, my navigator, was supposed to alert me to the exit that would take us to Cornwall, Ontario, but she fell asleep beside me and we continued, almost to the border crossing south of Montreal. We backtracked and, once we were across the bridge and onto the 401, lapsed into long, numbing, mute stretches. Their games of cards, I-Spy, song building and clapping and make-believe long since exhausted, the girls sat apart now in the back seat. I missed hearing them chatter and sing—it had kept me awake and attentive. Now the four-lane highway bore ahead inexorably with few diversions, the midsummer, eastern Ontario landscape burnt straw-brown, the vegetation as inspiring as bran.

Once we were in Toronto and off the freeway, I let out my breath. We arrived at my brother Wayne's house, unfolded our limbs from the stale-smelling car and agreed that we didn't care to sit in it another minute of our lives. We spent the first night with Wayne and the next with my sister-in-law Heidi, I on a foldout bed in the living room and the girls in a spare bedroom.

We met Heidi for lunch on King Street, near the office building where she worked. Burke, seated across the table from me and turned sideways in her chair, was speaking in a highly animated way to her aunt. Moll fumed over the menu because it didn't have anything she wanted or felt she was able to eat. Moll is allergic to nuts, and despite the waiter's assurance, that not one molecule of any variety of the dreaded fruit was used in the preparation of the cuisine, she was unconvinced.

"I may as well order a P.B. and J. and just get it over with," she said glumly from between the frame of her palms plastered to her cheeks.

To keep from laughing, which would have hurt and infuriated her, I looked over at a man and a woman seated beside and somewhat below us in a lower section of the restaurant. The man was Mate Speedwell, Victoria's husband before me. They got married as undergrads, but lasted only four years. They had no children together. She was married to him when she met me. Maitland Speedwell, named for his mother's family. Maitland Securities. He has some distant connection to the Molsons or the Eatons. One of those.

Had he looked up he would have seen me staring at him. If he had seen me earlier he wasn't indicating it. Rather, he continued to speak intimately with the woman, his lunch companion, in a low indistinct voice, smiling the smirk that men save for women they are trying to seduce. If this was a business lunch, it was in celebration of some recent or imminent union. Men make eyes like this at female colleagues and associates, but such looks are rarely consummated by the signing of papers. I felt feverish, my pulse, I was sure, visible in my neck.

Heidi leaned across and whispered, "Isn't that…?" I nodded.

"Isn't that who?" said rabbit-ears Burke.

"Do you want to leave?" I shook my head no and directed my attention to Moll, asking her to please put her Robert Munsch book down and pick something from the menu.

The waiter left and returned. Nothing would do. Moll was convinced that everything was going to make her sick. I had her EpiPen in my shirt pocket, but reminding her of it only made her more stubbornly afraid. Burke ordered what Heidi did, a pita wrap and a spinach salad. Spinach! We couldn't get her to say the word at home. Moll agreed to try a grilled cheese sandwich. Unlike Burke, she refused to be swayed by Heidi's poise and sympathetic voice. Burke studied the way Heidi wielded her fork, dabbed her napkin at her mouth between bites, sipped her iced tea. As I watched Burke watching Heidi, I was sure that Speedwell was watching all of us, but when I glanced over and down he was still locked in a *tête-à-tête* with his lunch companion.

When Heidi asked her how the road trip had gone so far, Burke gave an account of my strange behaviour at the motel. Heidi leaned into it, giving me a conspiratorial half-smile from the side. She was charmed by my daughters to the point of distraction, silliness or at the very least a limited kidnapping: her plan was to take them shopping for clothes after lunch and leave me on my own for a few hours, to give "old Dad" some time to himself. Burke took delight in my discomfort as she told the first part of her story. It wasn't the story that was making me flushed and fidgety. What if he recognized me? The girls didn't even know he existed. He was everything I wasn't: rich, successful, athletic, brawny with a water-polo player's chest and shoulders. Victoria had spoken his name three times since April. I was convinced that she regretted leaving him for me.

"So we pull into the parking lot and you'll never guess what the motel is called."

"The Moose—"

"No, I'm telling it."

"The Moose is Loose!"

"Dad!"

"Let her tell it, Moll."

It was indeed The Moose is Loose Motel outside of East Newport, Maine. Our room looked freshly made up, the covers on the two double beds smooth, the fold between the pillows and the rest of the bed crisp. The air was confused by old smoke, disinfectant, body odour and freshener in a piney, astringent waft. The girls held their noses while I squatted in front of the air conditioner.

"That better work," said Moll.

"Yeah. Or else."

"Or else what?"

"Or else I'm sleeping in the car."

"That I would pay money to see, Burke."

"How much, Daddy?"

I turned the knob, and the machine coughed and blew.

"It needs a muffler," said Moll, reminded of the way the car had suddenly become incorrigibly loud one day not long before the trip.

I sat on the end of the bed and aimed the remote control at the television set, a massive piece of baroquely carved cabinetry atop a long low chest of drawers.

"Aren't you going to unpack?" Burke, the voice of order. Little Victoria.

"Yes, in a minute."

Their clothes and toiletries were in two soft-sided carry-alls that resembled the cylindrical canvas bag I used to transport my ice-hockey equipment in. Burke unzipped theirs and began to divide their things and transfer them to separate drawers in the dresser. Moll complained that she wanted to keep her clothes in her bag and near her. Their quarrel had scant fuel. In the late-afternoon swampy heat, somewhere in New England, Old America, after ten hours of inactivity, they were holding each other accountable for their complicity in the demoralizing enterprise, and bolstering each other as well, for Victoria wasn't there, again, and it *was* different with me. Openings, possibilities and negotiations closed quicker. I suspect I made the world both shrink and expand for them, neither change being pleasant or desirable. What were the choices? Was there not a process in place? Wasn't I, the attendant adult, supposed to intervene at this point? When Victoria was with them they didn't have such terrible silences. With her they had the sensation of being able to see around bends; the straight lanes I sent them down probably seemed endless, receding to a harsh point of light.

When she saw that I wasn't going to do anything, Burke sighed and cut off further contention by returning Moll's things to her bag.

I should have turned the TV off, opened my own luggage, seen to my daughters' needs and, at least in a cursory, figurehead sort of way shown them that the authority vested in me, as impotent as it was, still existed. It was what they wanted. But what did I want? To be no longer tired but also to stay awake, to scan the century of channels for something extraordinary. I flipped through to the end and began the futile exercise again. The girls, who at home would have been content to flop beside me on their tummies, took long turns using the washroom. They cleaned their faces and hands, brushed their hair, and changed into fresh T-shirts.

I pulled the damp fabric away from the skin of my back and wondered if they could smell my yeasty funk. Was I tolerable? Were they disgusted? This was something to examine, bridge of the nose furrowed, eyebrow arched, before tucking it away into the archive. The Adult Male: What to Expect.

Burke drew the story out with what I could see were, for her, delicious asides and meandering tangents, for she was at that age when the path could be as desirable as the destination. She rolled her eyes for emphasis, employed hyperbole sparingly.

It was as if I had been under an evil spell, she said. "He sat there totally zonked for like an hour. You'll never believe what it took to get him moving again."

I had been sitting on the end of my bed, scanning channels with the sound off, when a knock sounded at the door. It was just dark, sometime after nine. Moll and Burke had got in under their covers and were beginning to doze. I got up, crossed the floor, put the end of the security chain into its bracket on the jamb, and opened the door as much as it would allow. Under the yellowish, fly-speckled globe of the outdoor light, the face peering up at me was male, of late middle-age, ruddy. The top of his head came to about the level of my shoulders and despite the heat he wore a white-and-blue V-neck tennis sweater.

"How's everything tonight, sir?"

"Fine," I said.

"Passing through, are you?"

"That's right. Is there a problem?"

"Oh, no. No. Can't say there's that. *Per se.*"

"*Per se?*"

"Who is it?" said Burke.

"Sounds like you have a minor in there with you in the room."

"Just what exactly do you want? Are you with the motel?"

"Do you like birds, mister?"

"What do you mean, do I like birds?"

"Dad, just close the door."

"It's okay, honey. Go back to sleep."

"We can't sleep," said Moll. "I want Mom."

"I was thinking I could come in and read you my poem. It's about a cormorant. I've read this poem in public over a hundred times. Are you familiar with the cormorant?"

"Yes, I am. And no, I don't think it would be a good idea. So goodnight. I'm sorry."

Before I could close the door, he inserted his arm in the opening.

"Your daughter might like to hear it. Are you a bird lover, daughter?"

"Now look here!" When I tried pushing his arm out, he thrust his foot in and hooked it around the bottom of the door. He squatted, jamming as much of the right side of his body as he could into the opening, fighting against my hand. The chain strained, taut, as if it was going to break. Both girls yelped when a sheaf of loose-leaf pages covered with immature handwriting in pencil flew in, as if blown by the wind, and settled haphazardly on the rug. I leaned my shoulder into the door heavily, angrily.

"Mercy!" he called out. "You're killing me! Stop!"

"Get out! Just get out!" I rammed the edge of the door against him repeatedly, not caring if I broke bones. He cried out with each blow. Finally he withdrew, first his arm and then his leg. I slammed the door shut and locked it.

I called the front desk to tell them what had happened.

"Where is he now?" said the night manager, who sounded like a younger version of the intruder.

"How should I know? The guy should be locked up."

"Oh, that's just George. Don't mind him. He goes off his nut sometimes in the heat. He's harmless."

"He tried to force his way into the room!"

"Did he read you his poem?"

"What? No. Why would I let him do that?"

"It's a good poem."

I hung up on the man and called the number for the police that I found in the directory. I gathered the scattered pages from the floor, ripped them up without reading them and stuffed them into the garbage can in the bathroom. Half an hour later I was giving a description of the man to a state trooper. He stood in the entrance, his starched blue Stetson grazing the top of the door frame as he jotted details in a small spiral notebook. The officer gave no indication that he knew who the crazy bird-poet was. The only thing I remember him saying was that the cormorant was not welcome in those parts. They crapped over everything and depleted Sebasticook Lake of sport fish.

At this point in Burke's narrative, Speedwell turned his head. We exchanged a brief glance, whether of recognition on his part I couldn't tell. It might have been the kind of look one parent gives another, acknowledging a child's achievement, a "you should be proud" kind of nod.

"Did they ever catch the guy?" he asked Burke, who looked flustered to have an unintended audience. I nodded to let her know it was all right to respond.

"We don't know. He sure scared us. I mostly feel sorry for him."

"A friend of mine once ran over a cormorant with his outboard. Totalled the motor," he said.

"Was it okay? Was the bird okay?" said Moll, her eyes welling.

"I don't imagine it was."

Moll began to sob. Speedwell's companion got out of her chair, came over and crouched beside Moll. "Hey, don't cry. He doesn't know what he's talking about. I was there. That bird flew off. It was perfectly fine, not a feather out of place." She opened her purse and took out a small packet, a white paper napkin with a pink ribbon tied around it. "How would you like a piece of wedding cake?"

"She can't if it has nuts in it. She's allergic," said Burke.

Rather than accentuate her sorrow, this announcement stopped Moll's tears. With the patience of one revealing her entitlement to a less fortunate person, she explained that if she ate it she could die.

"Better not chance it, then. Put it under your pillow and it'll give you sweet dreams."

"Congratulations, by the way," said Heidi.

"Oh, it wasn't us," said the woman, glancing at Mate. "A friend of mine. She got married last week."

"So she offers week-old unrefrigerated wedding cake to a kid with nut allergies. Brilliant."

"I was just trying to be nice, Matty. Sorry. Jeepers."

"So. How's Vicky?" he said, turning his attention to me.

I thought I was steeled for this question and the wreckage of its implications, but it felt like an unexpected blow to the side of the head. I hadn't been watching the boom as we went about.

"Pardon?"

"Victoria. Your wife?"

"Why do you ask?"

"Well, let's see. I don't know. I used to be married to the woman?"

"What are you doing here, Mate? Heidi told you we'd be here. You did, didn't you. You set this up."

Burke and Moll, wide eyed, looked ready to cry.

"Rob, get a hold of yourself. Lower your voice. I had no idea he'd be here."

"Look at him. Look at him sitting over there with his…"

"With my what?"

"Nothing. It doesn't matter." Now everyone in the restaurant was looking at me. The woman returned to their table, picked up her purse and waited for Mate to stand. He laughed, almost a bark, and shook his head. On his way out he turned around and said, "You give her my best."

"I will do nothing of the sort. She's getting nothing from you through me." I'd intended to stop at "I will."

"What is your problem?" he said, looking from me to Heidi as if to say, Get help with this one.

When the couple was gone, Moll said, "I don't like that man one cayuga."

"Who was he, Dad? Was what he said, was that true?"

I should have been figuring out what to say to my daughters in explanation and to my sister-in-law in apology. Instead, the following is roughly what passed through my mind:

Victoria married Maitland Speedwell on his uncle's 150-foot yacht, the *Swiftsure*, anchored in Montego Bay.

In 1620 a ship named the *Speedwell* was supposed to accompany the *Mayflower* to the New World, but twice it had to turn back to England because it began taking on seawater.

Boats make Victoria queasy.

The *Speedwell's* crew created the leaks in the hull because they wanted out of their contract.

You never hear about pilgrims not reaching their destination.

She got sick from a bad sunburn on her first honeymoon.

We exchanged vows in my parents' living room in Oakville.

Our honeymoon was a cool, overcast week spent hiking in the Adirondacks.

I remember feeling guilty that I'd taken the time off work.

One of the partners I used to work for said that history was whatever he deemed it to be.

Victoria bought her clothing store with money from her divorce settlement.

She threw her cell-phone down the slope when she couldn't get a signal from the top of Mt Marcy.

She admitted that she married Mate despite knowing that he was immature and a skirt chaser and immune to commitment.

Victoria's store would not exist without Speedwell money.

What if I make a lousy teacher?

Becalmed is better than storm-tossed.

Maybe. Maybe not.

THE GODDESS
THROWS DOWN

THE GODDESS
THROWS DOWN

She of No Further Forbearance surveyed her closet, wondering what to take, what to leave.

"The only hope," muttered Clyde, her husband, the big faker. "The children. Survival."

"You got that last part right, Mister-Less-Than-Nothing," She was a nurse practitioner in gerontology and she was heading way south of 49 to a pleasant enclosure of zero humidity near Phoenix where the average age was three score and twenty, and no one but the black-visored security angels at the gated perimeter wore leather holsters, and snow was a coned confection or the shade of white tufting the leathery pates nodding in desert bliss.

He mewed pathetic sounds at her leaving. "We had our moments, Marie-Ange."

"You had the moments."

"Shouldn't we talk about this?"

"Talk to the mirror. Talk to your *triplets*."

"But you and I could be role models to hundreds. Thousands. The young need what we can impart. Don't emigrate to the geezers, Marie-Ange. They ride their wheelchairs, shuffle behind their walkers, they're poised at the lip of the grave. They don't need you. They've had their poke. Look the other way. We could be saviours of many, teaching them how to thrive in a careless world. All the old kindnesses are gone."

She screwed her face into a mask of distaste, as much for his arcane expressions of passion as for his plan, which made her want to torture him with a departing slap, a flash of her bare muff, perhaps, before striding childless down the path, her baggage on the wheel.

Lest we be compelled to snuffle in sympathy for this man, Clyde Brind'amour, who once guarded the prime minister, we should know that by the third minute after the big yellow taxi took away his old lady, Clyde was on the land line to his secret honey, his newfoundgirl, Miss Donna Farr.

"Blessed Mother of Survival," he cooed. "The way lies open," as if the Goddess Herself had blazed a clear-cut through obfuscatory brush. "Darling, you with your culinary flare, your genius for stone soup, outport-style, and I with all knowledge of rescue and shelter-making and extracting poison from the serpent's bite, will be the perfect one-two. Throw in some edible plants, some water ballet in a canoe. Have I or have I not secured the perfect spot for the assumption of the Dream?"

Donna, the proverbial handful, thought his dream was to build a casino and make them both quickly rich, no waiting. Not only was she misinformed about that, in the eyes of many she was Clyde's professional undoing, a fetching drug mule he had had the pleasure to apprehend as she passed through Customs on her way home from Jamaica, and, instead of letting her pass naively through the churning digestive system of the courts and the prisons, he'd worked a clever winking deal with an exhausted judge. As in, first-time offender claiming ignorance, comely in a Molly Malone buxom-barmaid sort of manner, she walked, and was soon in residence in a tiny basement apartment paid for out of Brind'amour's dwindling chequing account, the withdrawals from which Marie-Ange quickly discovered. Clyde tried limply to explain them away as being support for foster triplets living in Costa Rica. When she heard this she raised one of her sculpted eyebrows into a circumflex and thusly she remained, visibly piqued, until alternate arrangements were made for the rest of her life. Even as Clyde jigged his own greying caterpillars in anticipation of bucolic cohabitation with the youthful Bella Donna of Lesser Lung, he knew that, of the two women, his wife had more to offer the rosy cheeked campers who were going to fill, he was sure of it, all available bunks in each weeklong session at Camp Cattail on the Mississippi.

Not the continent-emptying *fleuve* but a snaky stream too interested in its own flanks to be going anywhere in a hurry southwest of Ottawa,

Ontario. Some civic wag had had a good knee-slap christening that one. Clyde put a down payment on a place, nonetheless, near the mill town of Lanark, though the property was nothing more from the look of it than the side of a wooded hill that had slumped, saturated with too much rain, and tumbled into the little river, creating a sandy spit and beach, and clogging the channel, but conveniently uprooting trees and undergrowth that had to be removed to make way for the camp.

Lucky Clyde had an instant work force: twelve of life's sweetness and hope, armed with Swede saws and machetes. Smile without shuddering, do try, at the spastic industry of it. The rain, so that it would not be forgotten, it and its formidable land-altering power, held on, and Clyde decreed that in a survival situation one would not enjoy instant shelter, would one. Working in the rain was not singing in the rain, he granted the taller and more articulate of them that much.

"Let me clarify one thing," he replied to the committee of grievance that materialized in yellow slickers and rubber boots one morning at the door of his office, one of two semi-permanent structures on the property, the other a similar construction-site trailer that served as kitchen and mess hall. "Know this, my children. One day, when you are sleek and prosperous and your progeny are protected behind safe high walls reinforced by electrocution and razor wire, not to mention highly competent security officers—a growth profession, let me be the first to point this out for your future—you will look back on these worthy days of learning and labour and you will thank your Uncle Clyde. Bless you, you are all my sons and daughters and nieces and nephews and I would not for the life of me or the loss of my liberty want to see you rendered helpless. So go now, return to your work. The Goddess has done most of it for you."

Said deity was throwing down on the county like a vigilante. It was as if a grudge keeper had been holding her water all winter and spring. The slope to the river resembled the work of a great wounded vindictive bear, one mean paw-swipe with extended claws scooping out a chute the width of a suburban street.

Meanwhile his Bella Donna set about crafting starchy miracles of cuisine on the two dollars per camper per day he allotted her for food. She knew that in the flow chart of scheduled activities his novitiates, training

for survival following the coming chaos—the secular end-times, the closing of the natural world by climate change, rendering some parts desert,
some flooded—were slotted to pass the first week to ten days clearing
brush. It was to be an educational timber operation, he had told the parents. Before a child limbed and sectioned a fallen tree he had to be able
to identify it, sketch its leaf, know its bark the way the blind read Braille,
and approximate the age to within ten years. Communion, he promised,
honest sweat, knowledge of edible plants in the wild. Campers would
sleep muscle-sore each night. They would learn what they could munch
and what to leave in the ground. They would practise hauling injured
bodies in stretchers up the sides of mountains. They would let the saw
blade do the work.

Enough deadfall, rubble, tangle and vine remained to be cleared that
the clean-up easily could have consumed the summer, the children learning nothing more than peasant skills. Many of them were too puny to be
of measurable aid in the project. At night snaky tendrils invaded their
dreams, wrapping around their soft white throats, while during the day
burdocks tormented them beneath their shorts and shirt collars. The
Citizen's Committee of Complaint was not deterred from its purpose, despite Clyde's contention that the work would set them free. They weren't
falling for that.

The damp negotiating team consisted of one Jason Hyatt Plimpton III,
age thirteen, Bostonian, diabetic and verbally combative, having been
tutored since birth in the rules of courtroom debate; Callie (dim. of
Callaghan) Monroe, christened by a father whose literary tastes ran to
moralizing urban realism and whose greatest entertainment was the delivery of life-altering practical jokes; and three littl'uns, twin boys and
a girl, all of whom had been promised candy to stand in support of the
spokes-couple, barrister-in-embryo Jason and Callie Monroe, a black
haired, mythical creature, the kind sent to the surface to entice sailors
overboard. She was fifteen, too old to be a camper. She acted as if she
knew that her time on dry land was going to be tragically brief. We have
work to do, her eyes seemed to say, and she wasn't thinking about any
primitive landscaping venture.

"You're treating us like slaves," Jason's clincher. Callie intervened only to remove the boy's faded Red Sox cap and brush the hair out of his eyes. Already she knew what a man like Cap'n Clyde responded to: the male voice, the female pout, not to forget the lip-moist smile, eyelash bat, hip shift, feline purr. And her own clincher? Oh, nothing less than a sigh the quality of a crystal bell.

While Jason presented the case for the exploited proletariat, Clyde watched Callie. She seemed to fill more space than someone of her petite stature should. He let less-than-avuncular notions drift in like the first red bloom of disaster. He excused himself, promising to take their concerns under advisement.

Donna Farr was near. He thought about her proximity as the very thing to save him from inappropriate lust, not that she was all that closer in years to his forty-eight than was the alluringly precocious Callie Monroe. When he reached the kitchen trailer, Donna made her needs immediately clear: if she did not receive a larger food buying allowance, more time off during the week, an assistant to wash the pots and dishes, and a bathtub of her own—"That's all for now, but you knows I'm coming back at you some soon with additionals"—he was going to lose her away down the road and he could kiss her shapely posterior *au revoir*. Some attention was due, in other words. Clyde heard this and his heart lifted as on a mechanical spring, so acutely sensitive was he to subtext. Attention would she receive, most assuredly. They retired to her tent.

On her foam mattress she looked up at him encouragingly, helpmeet-like, such a sincere and studied actress in the love role was she. How then was it possible that in this moment of supreme nakedness and honesty and accommodation the Monroe girl's face was superimposed over that of his Donna Rosa?

"This can't be right," he said.

"What can't?" She sat up, pushing him off her and an arm's length away. Why was passion so often a cube of smoke suspended within a four-bubble shape? You would think they were strangers the way she hid her bare parts from him. Now one thing Clyde had never been able to do successfully was to lie. He knew from his lawman training what gave the liar away—lines on the forehead, tremors of the eye and mouth—and he knew he could never master the muscles of his face well enough to pre-varicate convincingly. He was too simple, boyish, craven and unsophisti-cated ever to be a bad guy. And so he tried to say something else to go with his unfortunate utterance.

"I mean this, us, in the middle of the day, the innocent marshalled all around with their woodsman implements. Hungry. They will be want-ing their lunch soon, no?" He sniffed as if attempting a detection of cooking aromas.

Donna dressed angrily and in haste, and ducked out through the tent flap. He could hear her loud stomps taking her along the path to the mess trailer, from whence came the sound of rummaging in a drawer, metal cutlery ransacked and scattered across the plywood floor, and then the door making full backhanded contact with the outside wall. Two strides, it sounded like, and she was back. He was still lying on his side on her bed, listening. He rolled onto his back, smiled up at her.

At once bathed in an icy spray, he lost the air out of his lungs. Gasping intake of breath when he saw the lighter flame emanating from her raised fist: righteous avenging Liberty.

"You are some close to it, Clyde Brind'amour. One blink away, in fact. Don't blink."

One expression he could communicate, because he never had to try, was that of innocent incomprehension.

"I have requirements," she said.

"Understood."

"Changes will be made."

"Most definitely."

"You will join me in the kitchen. I am referring to you being a help to me, Officer Clyde. You may have saved me from a bad life, but I now have rising expectations, one of which is that never again will you refer to me as 'not right.'"

How the eyes of the bourgeoisie do rise above the horizon. Or was it the peasantry? He could not remember his high-school history lessons. Whichever it was, she had him: shivering, happy, on the verge of wet-ting himself. Again at the mercy of a woman. He promised, agreed to everything, including the hiring of outside workers to finish the clearing of brush. "Let these babies have some fun. You can't take their money and then turn them into drudges. It's downright Dickensian, this workhouse business. It has to stop."

Very well, he said. He also agreed to take as many of them as possible away somewhere for a few days. She would stay, oversee the clearing of the brush. The time was necessary to her sanity.

"Get the little capelin out of my hair. They're always Jesus hungry. I can't be held responsible for what I might do otherwise."

Again he promised, and as he did so he crossed his heart. Here was a woman prepared to burn him alive with her love. She was not one to run from his faulty regard, not with barely a shrug or a by-your-leave. He vowed to stop being miserly, to hire a couple of local men with chainsaws, to take a troop of campers away on a canoe trip, and to be more attentive to his fish-plant Venus.

In all they were eight paddlers, including himself, in three canoes: Jason, Callie, Waterfront Larry, who was the least obnoxious of the three counsellors, and four campers who had passed the basic test, which was to tip over into the water while in the canoe and not die. They strapped the boats onto a trailer, jammed some dried food into waterproof packs, and piled into the truck, inside and out. It was eighty kilometres by road to the headwaters of the questionable river. As she drove, Donna's smile broadened with every furlong.

"Good luck, Clyde. Don't get lost," she said when they disembarked.

"From your tone I detect that you might be wishing the contrary."

"Oh pooh, don't mind me. Need to be on my own for a few. Need to miss my constable. You understand."

Of course he did. He was already thinking of their reunion. The voyage would end at the camp beach, which with its dressing of deadfall still looked like a spot somewhere along the Amazon. Waterfront activities were creative and cautious, to say the least. Lifeguard Lawrence, to his credit, had cleared enough space that they could get into the water without having to climb over anything, and Clyde had plans to build a stationary raft they all could swim to. He hoped that by the time *les coureurs de bois* had returned, the place would look like a real summer camp.

Clyde watched Donna drive away, cringing as she spun the tires, gleefully it seemed, gravel rattling in the van's wheel wells, the empty boat trailer bouncing. Let her have her woman time, he thought. The reunion would be sweet. He pictured her waiting on an expanded and newly raked sand beach for him and his intrepid Argonauts. Sunburned would they be, strong paddlers having had so much practice, each stroke long and deep and powerful, second nature after so many twisting leagues. He would teach them Quebecois songs to maintain their spirits. He would amaze them with chilling but age-appropriate stories of his time on the force. Each evening around the campfire they would sit cross-legged to eat. How they would appreciate nourishment in the open air, feel each stroke in the shoulders, sleep the sleep of blissful exhaustion.

They prepared the canoes, loading their packs, evenly distributing the weight, matching the strong and the weak so that each boat would travel at much the same speed as the others. The day, the sky, the weather ahead: warm, clear, beckoning. "An auspicious day on which to embark," he announced. "A great day to test ourselves." Where Donna had let them off the river was low and rocky but deep enough that they could navigate the middle channel without hitting anything. Clyde took the two smallest children in his boat. They were twin blond brothers, nine years old, a pair of quiet angels he could not for the life of him get to say much more than yes, no, fine and okay. He set the pace, his J-stroke smooth, efficient. He did not have to put his back into it. The boys, one kneeling in the middle and the other in the bow, paddled on the same side to balance Clyde, and still he had to compensate. They took instruction well, obeying his command that they leave their hats on and fashion neck coverings with spare shirts against the sun. They kept pace with Larry's canoe, stopping every half hour or so for the other boat to catch up.

After the first ten kilometres the water level dropped and they began scraping the bottoms of the boats on the rocks. They had to get out and walk in the shallows, lifting the canoes up and over and around obstacles.

Clyde tried to bolster their flagging spirits. He didn't have to remind them that they were in this together, that none including he had ever been on a canoe trip before. He had trained in mountainous regions, where he rescued skiers from avalanches, flown in helicopters tracking marijuana growers, and completed a hundred-mile endurance walk over a three-day period, but had managed to miss this quintessentially Canadian experience.

They came to the first in a string of old mill-towns built along the waterway. After the slow meandering progress through marsh and weedy lake, over rocky shallow and through tricky chutes of rapidly flowing water—suddenly after long stretches of dry bottom came these torrents—to come upon such stone sedateness and pass like a small ceremonial flotilla under the granite archways, see the cryptic messages spray painted underneath where few eyes wandered, gave them renewed vigour.

At the same time, Donna was telephoning the parents of the remaining campers and telling them to collect their children. "Camp's closed. Toxic spill upriver." She dismissed the two remaining counsellors, telling them that Clyde would pay them when he returned. "Make sure we have your mailing address."

"But he promised to teach us how to skydive." They had been so looking forward to jumping out of a plane.

"You can still do that, bye. Sorry, no more work. What can I say? All the best to yous and good luck."

She packed her suitcase, pocketed Clyde's credit cards, and drove in a westerly direction to seek her fortune in a manner more conducive to personal gain and happiness. Camp Cattail, empty but for two young men, the locals Clyde had hired to finish clearing the deadfall, awaited the intrepid paddlers, still a day away.

How quiet at dusk the swath running down to the water's edge, the two trailers left unlocked, the children's tents on their plywood floors sitting like sentinels set back in the woods. The clean-up crew, two princes of destruction, roamed the empty camp. They had grown up in the town but had not outgrown the meanness they had ingested with their first gulps of mother's milk. Inbred youths who would never know the joy of Kumbaya, Smores, Morning Dip, Arts & Crafts, and Woodland Lore, they sneered like garbage-dump bears lurching through the cleared spaces of Clyde's dream. The tents came down, their canvas reduced to shredded tatters in seconds, courtesy of the boys' sharp knives. They found Donna's naphthalene and in their estimation put it to excellent use, turning the trailers into handsomely blazing pyres.

Clyde and his *voyageurs* paddled with the strengthening current, a slight breeze against them. Donna drove the Trans-Canada through Northern Ontario, which she deemed cruel in its endless coniferous monotony. She vowed to send Clyde a postcard from the first town she reached in Manitoba. It would say, "Thanks & love, Clyde. Free woman b/c of you. So glad you didn't blink." The hopeless arsonists watched the campsite smoulder from a far-off hill and punched each other until they could no longer lift their arms. The river widened and deepened. In the lulling sunshine Clyde watched water drip hypnotically off the end of his paddle. In turn he thought about each of his young companions, loving them for who they were and what they knew, what they didn't yet, what he'd tried to teach them. He was but a rickety footbridge they had already crossed with no backward glance in their flight from innocence. The way they looked at each other, surreptitiously, cramped with love-ache, openly like tethered siblings, outraged by the others' presence—he saw it all. He would give them everything if he could.

HIGH HARD

HIGH HARD

"IT IS THE FATE of a living creature… that it cannot secure what belongs to it without an adventure in a world that as a whole it does not own and to which it has no native title."

—*John Dewey*

PRADESH HAD INVESTED well and weekly we would learn to the nearest thousand dollars how much he was worth. He took impish pleasure reminding us that he had more in real property and stock shares than did the ten wealthiest of us frayed, unravelling teachers lumped together. That he continued to work as the custodian of our crumbling but venerable school, Monsignor Clarence Cleary Collegiate, given his purported ability to retire at any time (he was not yet forty) might confound some, but I think I understood him. It was as if he were a rough-hewn prince who did not dare distance himself from an educated subclass of his serfs, whom he pitied for their status and struggle but envied for their knowledge, because to leave would be to lose both an audience and an advantage, the latter of which registered in his mind alone. It was important we see him, regal, with his daily mop and pail, his ladder and tools, deigning to replace a fluorescent light tube, scrub graffiti off a rank of dented and scored hall lockers, or spread coarse salt and sand on the icy walkways of winter.

I didn't mind Pradesh, even liked him, as much as a chalky pedant like me could be friends with the man whose job it was to empty my garbage can at the end of the day. He was an important ally, especially when the heat went out in the classroom or when a student opened a window that subsequently refused to close or, as one once did, caused it to fall out, shattering on the pavement three floors below.

One of our colleagues who saw Pradesh but remained oblivious to his overweening self-regard was young Hal Malvern, a newly minted teacher who taught history and economics. If you've never heard of the Malverns, you probably don't read newspapers, listen to radio or watch local television stations in this part of the world. The patriarch, Godslave Malvern, initiated the dynasty as a printer of advertisements and broadsheets in 1833. By the time the Malvern boys of my father's generation came along, there wasn't much for them to do except collect dividends and interest, instilling in none of them any sort of drive to better himself, the business being by that time a nation-wide printing operation run by an army of experts.

Our Hal was a recent graduate of Cleary (he went on to be nicknamed "High Hard" by his college fraternity), and having heard from birth that essentially he would one day *be* the family business he shocked his parents, the company's board of directors and the major shareholders with the announcement that he intended to teach. As a comparative disappointment and potential setback, this news rivalled both the labour strife of 1988 and the massive loss of revenue suffered by the company, Malvern, Inc., in 1995. He had made his family vulnerable to ridicule. There was no reasoning with him. What can one say to someone so green and headstrong? Undeterred, he made do with a reduced allowance, a pittance compared to what his younger brother now received as the new dauphin.

When Hal arrived his first day on the job, I noticed that Pradesh paid particular attention to the well-dressed rookie as he passed through the crowded halls. Hal appeared both eager to please and confident that he would succeed in doing so, turning heads with his casual, athletic good looks. Female students and the younger women on staff quickly came to adore the preppy new instructor. To them he was not "Hard" but "High Handsome," and the intensity with which some of them scrutinized his speech and deportment, his endearing quirks and mannerisms, approached silliness. Just as he seemed to be blind to Pradesh the janitor tycoon, Hal appeared not to be aware that he was the object of crushing affection for so many in his midst.

Distanced from his family's wealth and earning only a modest salary, Hal rented a ground-floor apartment in a house near the school. It was affordable and he could walk to work in ten minutes. His landlord was a simple minded, underemployed bachelor who lived upstairs. The walls and ceiling of Hal's two-rooms-and-a-bath were thin and not insulated, and he could hear every footstep, every mumble uttered by John Robert, as the man called himself, the first and last name run together like a reversible windbreaker.

Pradesh knew this man, John Robert, because the custodian had once had his eye on the house as a rental investment and had actually out-bid the eventual buyer, he would later learn. Realtors handled the transaction, ownership was transferred from the unidentified, winning bidder to John Robert and his sister, and officially no evidence of racial prejudice was ever admitted.

The opportunity to strike came one day when a cousin of Pradesh, a records clerk at city hall, let it slip that John Robert was going to have his property seized for non-payment of taxes. All because John Robert's sister, who answered the mail and handled the bookkeeping, had moved away to marry a man she had met online, leaving her brother ignorant of his responsibilities and obligations. Her last words to him were that he should hire an accountant to keep up with the payments on the property. She would send him a few hundred a month, but the rental income, from Hal and from the only other tenant, a reclusive older man who inhabited the top floor, she assured him would be enough to live on.

John Robert remembered his sister's instructions for a period of one day. Then all he could remember was that there was something important he was supposed to do. For a few weeks the urge to recall what it was subsided, until a heavy rain revealed that the roof was leaking, at which damp and contentious moment John Robert said his equivalent of "Eureka!" and proceeded to do what he did best, which was to scoot on up to the building-supply store to buy tar paper, roofing shingles and nails. A week later, proud of his handiwork, he called the dumpster-rental company to take away the old shingles and roof board. Remembering at last his sister's directive he delivered a stack of unopened mail, everything that looked as if it might be a bill, to an accountant recommended by the man who ran the building-supply franchise. But the accountant, an elderly man of my parents' vintage, caught the flu and died in hospital of pneumonia before he could get to John Robert's bills. The city sent notice after notice, eventually seizing the property for non-payment of taxes. The house was put up for auction, and who of all people do you suppose got wind of the sale in time to pick up the place for considerably less than what it was worth?

It tickled Pradesh no end to be the new owner of a property he considered morally if not legally his prior to the seizure and auction. He didn't drive, but knew that I did and that I had a free period before lunch. Vindicated, triumphant, requiring an audience, he could wait no longer to claim his prize. We sat conspicuously in my car on the street in front of the house, while John Robert and another, younger man, his sister's son by a previous marriage, loaded furniture and boxes into a large rental truck. Either unwilling or unable to write his two tenants a note explaining the change, and too proud to ask his nephew to do it for him, he emptied all the rooms except Hal's and the top-floor apartment. Hal Malvern was at that moment trying to explain, with less effectiveness than he thought, the mercantile system to a group of grade ten history students who were suffering from low blood sugar. Who knows what the old fellow who lived in the attic was thinking or doing.

Pradesh looked impatiently at his watch. He could take no more time watching his new possession being emptied of what was evidently a pile of junk. He had to return to the school. His pager could buzz at any time. Endless was the list of disasters that could befall "the physical plant," as he preferred to call the school. But it mattered extravagantly that this illiterate bohunk see him, Sarish Pradesh, the new owner. More than anything he wanted to walk up the path, pass by the departing diminished man, say not a word in greeting, and enter the property that was now rightfully his.

Before Pradesh could accomplish this, however, the fool drove away, not even glancing in his side-mounted rear-view mirrors as he did so.

PRADESH WAS ONE to appease, accommodate, listen to with one ear open while I scrambled to prepare for a class or dreamt about a rewarding drink at the end of the day. I was often making up a lesson on the fly while he yakked, invariably, about wealth. He had known hardship in the country of his birth. Never again would he go hungry or be forced to beg. I was a complacent grasshopper, he said. Didn't I know that the pension plans were emptying? Really, how much had I set aside? How quickly could I liquidate my assets?

That it was none of his business, that he presumed correctly the sorry state of my savings, and that I responded minimally usually did little to stem his monologue, but I could see him losing interest in me, my attitudes and lack of preparedness for the coming lean years, and shifting his attention toward his inherited tenant, young Malvern, who had been sleeping on the foldout couch in my den for the past three days and would continue to do so for another week until Pradesh completed extensive renovations—wiring, plumbing, structural improvements—required to bring Robert House up to code. People continued to call it Robert House, even after Pradesh won the auction. No one was sure what happened to the other tenant, the pensioner in the attic. Some said he went to live with a distant relation. Others perpetuated the rumour that an engineer found the man dead when he went up there to inspect the premises.

Although Pradesh was fascinated by Malvern's pedigree, and knew more about the success of that family's business concerns than was contained in your average annual report, he was not even mildly surprised that the young man chose to work for a salary. Work, regardless of kind or remuneration, was its own justification and reward, both a means and an end. Not to work was to move one's table down into the storm cellar and dine on emergency rations.

Double Hal's age and you have mine; divide his attractiveness and energy down the middle and you approached the reserves still available to me then. I knew twice what he did about teaching and yet his greenness could hardly have mattered less, to his students or his bosses. His magic, at least for the next few weeks—it began to wane predictably after Thanksgiving—was his naïve and thoughtless command of his students' attention. He had an ear for their vernacular and shared more than a passing knowledge of the cultural iconography they worshipped. More remarkable was that he could converse just as easily with my aged parents, who lived with me in a self-contained, ground-floor apartment attached to the house.

The Malvern pack had a sister, Katerina, who was the youngest of seven. I'm guessing she was born in the late 1930s. My father had a debilitating crush on Katerina in the sixth grade and it continued through their years together at Cleary Collegiate. He thought nobody knew about it, especially my mother, who was the one who told me. Poor boy in love with rich girl, a story timeless and mundane. The three oldest boys got most of the attention, doubtless their undoing. Their children built the company into the media conglomerate it is now. I don't know much about the other three of my father's generation, a boy and two girls. I assume they turned out all right, because you don't hear them mentioned.

The school was celebrating its hundredth birthday the year Hal started teaching there, and the administration sent word to all alumni it could find. My father didn't want to be found, he said when I showed him the letter. He stopped giving the school his change of address years before because it seemed to him that all they wanted from him was his money, and he was right. Go after the glorious Malverns, he said, even within earshot of Hal.

"That gang could pay off the national debt if it wanted to. They already own everything," he would complain, not that Daddo was hurting. He made out fine after he quit working as a chemist for Malvern, Inc. and concentrated on his own patents. You had to hand it to the old cat. As soon as he stopped griping about other people benefiting from his hard work, and stepped off the treadmill, everything changed. The company tried to claim his first invention, a non-smudging ink, as theirs, maintaining that it had been created in their labs. We're lucky that Uncle Jack, Mim's brother, is one sharp litigator. My parents have a retirement fund thanks to him.

Getting that reminder from the school must have set Daddo to thinking about Katerina and sinking into pathetic nostalgia. She got involved romantically with a couple of fellows in her late teens, not at the same time, but close enough one after the other that the gossip was flying for a few years. Rumour had it that she was living with the second man, an artist who was having a difficult time making a living, when she went back to be with the first, whom she eventually married. Anybody, housepainter, truck driver, hobo, who married into the Malvern family was set for life, and so it couldn't have been about money. What I mean is that her going back to the man who would become her husband had to have been about something else. I've often wondered what motivates people in the romance department once the problem of making money is no longer that, a problem. This probably shows the vastness of my ignorance, but I always thought that women who were inclined that way, toward men, looked for something strong and bright in him, good genes, good looks, the right family, no madness troubling dark corners. So it's always been a head-scratcher for me to think about Katerina Malvern taking up with big-eared, snaggle-toothed Gordon "Bats" Choppinghurst, leaving him, and returning to marry him after having been with the man everybody knew she passionately loved.

Katerina Malvern. Mention that name and, unlike his vociferous reaction whenever I would mention Choppinghurst, whom he considered dead weight, Daddo clammed. I learned to wait until he had gone to bed before asking my mother to tell me more about the Malvern-Choppinghurst intrigue. There was a pretty long time covering most of my growing up when she wouldn't say much of anything about that family or their business. It wasn't polite to gossip. Daddo wouldn't approve. She didn't remember. It was so long ago. Why was I buzzing around asking her about such nonsense? Didn't I have papers to grade? It may have been the icy breath of advancing years on the back of her neck or the presence of a Malvern in the house, because gradually she became much more talkative about such matters.

Her memories emerged piecemeal in the evenings and weekend afternoons, and I learned to be patient. She wasn't as quick as she used to be. Some days she had nothing new to reveal, plying me with stories I knew so well they were part of my repertoire of dreams. Some days she seemed to contradict herself, forcing me to resort to subtle cross-examination. For example, she insisted that Katerina Malvern had been her best friend in school and that the friendship ended when each set her sights on Daddo. According to Mim—I have doubts about this part of the story, since the first person she ever told it to was my houseguest, Hal Malvern—she knew that Daddo had a thing for the rich girl and she stepped between them before anything serious could transpire.

When I asked her about this "Bats" character she smiled. You can believe there was dissembling mischief behind those twinkling eyes. Choppinghurst. Of course, there's the famously philanthropic Choppinghurst Foundation and its support of the arts, begun and fuelled with Malvern millions, but what about Bats? I know that people of that generation used to go in for crazy nicknames. It had something to do with trying to blow fresh air into the atmosphere of sombre formality that followed the end of the war. Sure, everybody knew there was work to be done, no kidding. It was a time to rebuild the world and get rich and never let anything like that foreign horror happen again. But you couldn't keep a corset on all day, could you. In the after hours you donned your moniker, your *nom de jeu*, changed out of business attire and it was, Break out the cocktails, gang! In a sense, given the times and the mood and the countervailing current of restlessness, any poor schlub saddled with the name Choppinghurst had no choice but to be Bats.

I asked Mim to fill me in on the details, as in, who was this Bats and why did Katerina return to him after she had her fling with the painter? You would think that I'd asked her to derive special relativity. It's too complicated. I can't remember. Keep your voice down. Your father's sleeping.

I finally did sort it out. "You have to picture your father in the sixth grade," she said. "That's where you have to begin." She dug in the bottom drawer of a bureau and pulled out a photo album. Normally when Mim and I get into the photo albums it's an entire day lost. This time I was on a mission and she had already made so many false starts in the story that I wasn't going to be sidetracked reminiscing about summers spent up with the cousins on Lost Moose Lake. But she was determined to show me something.

"There," she said, stabbing a plastic-covered page with her finger. "There they are." It was a class photo in black and white, a formal pose of thirty or so children arranged in three rows, the first standing on a gymnasium floor and the two behind it on risers. I'd seen it many times. Miss Jesperson's grade-six class, 1942. "That's your father and that's Katerina beside him."

"Okay. So?"

"So look! Look at their hands."

The image was blurry and it took the magnifying glass to reveal it, but there indisputably was the girl's left clasped in the boy's right. And there at the bottom of the picture were their names.

I AM BY nature reclusive, an odd confession for a teacher to make. Sometimes I think that when I retire and Daddo and Mim are gone, I'll leave the house only when not to do so will mean starvation or Vitamin D deficiency. I see online shopping to be a boon to my late adulthood. Delivery people will come to know that I will always be home to answer the door and sign for parcels destined for my neighbours. I will tip generously, as if by handing over the money I will ensure the continuity of my hermitage.

You can be sure I wanted to shut all doors and windows and keep my head down the day Prince Hal interceded to return John Robert to his former home. I heard about it on the ninth of the ten-business-day grace period that had begun with Robert House being seized and sold at auction. Apparently John Robert had a two-week legal window through which he could crawl back into possession of his lost property.

The bell had just rung to mark the change of classes and here was Pradesh thrashing Coho-like against the stream, which was an egress of subversively variant uniforms: sassily short kilts, skater-baggy grey flannels and rumpled, knee-length white dress shirts. He waited until the last student had left before closing the door.

"They'll wait only so long out there," I said, nodding in a reassuring way to the puzzled faces peering in through the little window in the door. "Then I have to go out and lasso them."

"This will not take long," he said. To judge by his expression, civilization itself was doomed and I was to blame. He informed me that my protégé and houseguest had taken it upon himself to pay the outstanding taxes and residual fees pertaining to the property. Pradesh's property. The house he had won fairly at auction. Reprieve for an undeserving simpleton. Furthermore, ignominy heaped upon insult, Pradesh would have to wait thirty days for a refund, minus a considerable processing fee. "I am poorer because of that man. Do you hear me? Poorer!"

It was no use trying to argue innocence. Pradesh said, "I tell you this so that you are apprised. I know you are not to blame. You will inform Master Malvern for me, please, that from this moment and for all time he and I will no longer be in direct communication."

I fulfilled my role as intermediary twice that year, once to tell Hal that his students were not to place plastic or glass items in the recyclable-paper blue-box, and again to ask the young teacher to ensure that the windows of his classroom were closed before he left the building each Friday. Pradesh could just as easily have written a note, but I wasn't about to quibble. It was important that I be seen supporting him in this subservient way. It didn't last. After two years of teaching, Hal went back to university to earn a doctorate. The last I heard of him he was a professor of education at a university out on the west coast.

John Robert and his sister, I learned from Mim, were the children of Katerina Malvern Choppinghurst and her lover, the artist, a man named Jared Allen Robert, whose paintings remain obscure, collected only by those few who think that the Malvern connection will some day make them valuable. A dour aunt and uncle of the artist, unmarried siblings, raised the children on a rubble-strewn farm, and Mim was convinced that the boy, John, grew up emotionally and socially retarded due to lack of affection. As difficult as it was to believe, Katerina would have nothing to do with her children, even after Choppinghurst offered to embrace them as his own. Childless, they bred short-tempered Kerry Blue terriers, attended galas and administered the Foundation.

"Well that doesn't seem all that complicated," I said to Mim. "What was so difficult about telling me that?"

"I don't know. It has to do with what might have been, I suppose. Your father and I spend most of our conscious time now thinking about the past. I mean, Katerina. Your father has her sealed in amber, the very model of innocence and perfection. Are we ever better, really, in the ways that matter, than when we are eleven years old? And me—shoot, I can't help thinking about what you would have been like as a Malvern. You see, if I hadn't stepped in between Katerina and your Daddo—"

"Now are you sure about that?" I said. "You really were her best friend in school, no fooling? I thought that was just one of your stretchy stories."

"Oh, no, it's the truth. How could it have been otherwise? Think about it," she said, squinting at me as if I were a quickly fading photograph. "You only have to consider the implications."

"Katerina Malvern had eyes for Daddo?"

"I don't appreciate your tone."

"Just look at him. He was never any Adonis." I should know; I'm his younger double.

"She married Gordon, didn't she? Where do you think he got his nickname from, a predilection for caves?"

She was becoming distracted, sad and irritable about the eyes, her features slackening, as if her youthful act of intervention were now meaningless. Although a long shot, my father might well have married an heiress. Could he have competed with the shadowy painter, Jared Allen Robert? I tried to picture Daddo in the role of aggressive suitor. I replayed what I knew or thought I knew, the assembled details and, overlaid, alternative layers.

"You just couldn't help spill all this to young Hal, could you," I said.

"What's that, dear?"

"I'm referring to what Hal did to Pradesh."

"I'm sure I don't know anything about that."

"I'm sure you don't."

"Some people don't know their place."

"Excuse me?"

"Who do you think bought Robert House for that helpless twit and his sister to live in?"

"I have an inkling, but why don't you tell me, Mim?"

"What's the fun in that?"

"A man was cheated out of his property! What's the fun in that?"

"Malverns have always taken care of their own. The sooner your friend…"

She fell asleep mid-utterance. I switched off the television, covered her with an afghan, and went into their bedroom to say goodnight to Daddo, who was already dressed in his pajamas and dozing in bed. It was all of eight-thirty in the evening. I left a light on in the bathroom, locked the door behind me and retired, complicit, to my own dark rooms.

Hal Malvern returned to Robert House and lived there, with John Robert again overhead but less noisily so, until the end of the school year in June. I helped him move his furniture and belongings into a one-bedroom condominium that he'd bought downtown. He'd been given a modest raise in salary and some Malvern stock he owned had recently split. Soon after that, Pradesh quit working at the school and opened a convenience store in the heart of the business district.

I have a large painting hanging in my dining room. I keep meaning to get the portrait framed. Hal gave it to me the day I helped him move. When I asked him where it came from he said that John Robert presented it to him, as a token of thanks, with two other similar oils of the same subject. He had found them with dozens of others, some water damaged, all unsigned and stacked facing the sloping walls of a large storage cupboard in the attic apartment. Mine is of a seated young woman from the back. Her head is turned to her left so that we see her face in profile. Something or someone out of the frame has caught her attention. She's wearing a strapless, coral-coloured gown, low-plunging, individual vertebrae exposed. Her black hair is pulled back from her face and adorned with a silver comb in the Spanish style. In her left hand, dropping below the level of the chair, a furled forgotten fan. Her lips are pursed in a provocative pout. The eyelid we can see is heavy, as if beginning to wink, as if she knows that a certain wrong has been righted, influence brought to bear, a deal hushed, roughened matter wrought smooth with an aptly timed word.

HOT YOGA

HOT YOGA

△

THE ADDRESS 319 Griffen was known to cabbies and cops if not the public in general. Because ours was one number lower, we knew to tip well if we ever wanted to see a taxi in our vicinity again. But we liked the location and were getting to know our neighbours, and so we accepted the occasional outburst of deviant behaviour as both the price and reward of living an interesting life.

I would see all types pull up in front of 319, which was directly across from us: students, suits, bikers, skaters, soccer moms. The ones in the suvs would idle while a passenger dashed inside, never for more than a minute or two, and once I saw a kid no older than five run to the door, the bottom of which was scuffed and dirty where it opened at ground level. Because she couldn't reach the handle, she had to insert her fingers between the edge of the door and the jamb to open it. I know what you're thinking: I should have reported it. But let me ask you something. Have you ever lived somewhere and liked the house and the surroundings so much that you were willing to look the other way for the sake of your quiet enjoyment? We didn't want repercussions. I was afraid of being visited by someone less welcoming and solicitous of us than maybe we felt we deserved.

When we moved in I discovered that a man living at 319 was collecting welfare cheques addressed to him but delivered to our house. He had cleverly noticed that mail was being dropped between the doors of the vacant house—we had a mail slot installed soon after we moved in—and arranged to have his money sent there. I don't know what his relationship was with the woman who was dealing drugs out of her ground-floor apartment. I think he was living with her in a common-law arrangement, in which case neither of them could have been on the dole legally, given that they were fit to work, weren't raising small children, and didn't appear to suffer debilitating mental or physical ailments.

He arrived a few minutes after the mail carrier. It was unsettling to see a stranger standing between our storm door and main one, looking through our letters. Everything we received that morning was junk, but it was, as my father used to say, the bleeding principle of the thing. What right had he to paw invasively through correspondence addressed to us? Just as he removed the envelope he was searching for I opened the door and asked him what he thought he was doing. His response was so quick and reasonable that I assumed that I must be in the wrong. He said that he had given Social Services our street number by mistake and would be sure to change it right away. In the meantime, he said as he river-danced lightly down our front steps, if I wouldn't mind directing anything else with his name on it across the street or, even better, to hold it for him until he called again, he would be very grateful.

The next time we got a letter from Social Services addressed to Stewart Munce, I walked it in to their office and explained what had happened. Stewart, if that was his real name, came by a few times after that asking for his mail. Then a man and a woman dressed in dark suits arrived. They asked me some questions about Stewart and about the misdirected cheques and the reason why I had returned the last one. Apparently satisfied by my answers, they went away. I didn't see Stewart again until the night of Betty Camphor's literary soiree a few months later.

If a street is to transcend its questionable reputation, as Griffen Road did during those few years when we lived on it, it needs a resident like Betty Camphor, who lived beside the notorious 319. Betty didn't put up with shit from anybody. It didn't matter if she was dealing with precious university types like us or the troglodyte who got herself taken down, along with a scrawny associate in a leather Johnny Reb cap, in a midsummer raid at dawn that saw six cruisers fill our block, all of them lit and vibrating. As the cat and I watched through the slats of the bamboo shade covering our bedroom window, the stake-out and eventual arrest progressed unhurriedly, like a mannered, encoded drama filmed in French in Saigon in the early 1950s.

Betty bought her house after her husband ran off with a much younger woman. Back then, eighteen years ago now, the neighbourhood was an even less desirable a place to live than it is now, populated by former prison inmates and their families. A group of prostitutes used to operate out of the house we moved into. Spent syringes and condoms littered the back parking-lot. It was a complete starter-kit of antisocial behaviour then, a period we just missed experiencing. Despite all that, Betty loved her house. It had a solid foundation, was well built and affordable, and she admitted that she got a shiver of satisfaction knowing that her ex-husband, with whom she had remained close, had to worry about her safety in that dodgy part of town.

When we met I gave her a copy of my first book, the one about doctors and their secret lives, the intersection of unrealistic expectation and unforgiving reality. The book, a thin collection of stories, got some short-lived attention. A reviewer wrote that mine was a name to watch for, whether in avoidance or welcome I couldn't be sure. Another wrote that although I was no Alice Munro I had a knack for creating quirky characters. Betty read it in an evening, returned it the next day and informed me that her ex-husband was also a writer. That's like saying that a psychiatrist and a street-corner pusher fill the same essential need. Bernard Camphor was the sort of writer who produced a major book every five years. They were rarely shorter than six hundred pages, not that length is the measure of literary excellence. Look at *The Double Hook* or *Heart of Darkness*. My own modest output amounted to two collections of short fiction, some poems in an anthology and a humour book about the spirituality of cats that continues to sell well enough that I can keep writing with considerably less guilt than I might otherwise. Writers in isolation can convince themselves of just about anything, given how much of their day is spent inside their own heads. I have convinced myself, for example, that I am actually making it as a writer, despite knowing that without Deborah's salary I would be no better off and probably worse than Stewart Munce, astute observer of temporarily empty houses, grabber of timely opportunity. Furthermore, remind a writer that others do what he toils at and better, considerably so, with greater monetary reward and larger notice and critical praise he can only dream of receiving, and the illusory bubble soon bursts.

"Bernie was over while I was reading it," she said. "I read him the first story, the little one about the husband who joins the hot-yoga class and he's the only man? He got quite the laugh out of it. He was very interested to know that I have another writer living across the street from me. It's been a while since I've seen him so perked up by anything going on in this neighbourhood. Do you know what he calls it? *La Banlieue*. I don't think he's using it in a complimentary way, do you?"

The story she read him wasn't meant to be funny. I guess that's less disturbing than the knowledge that someone of Bernard Camphor's stature should have chuckled, no doubt derisively, over something I wrote. I would rather he had never known who I was, but the toad had found its way into the bread bag, as my dear departed father used to say.

I would watch Betty sweeping, raking or shovelling, according to the season, and get glimpses of the beauty who, forty years ago, was living, newly married to Bernard, in graduate-student accommodations at Stanford, where he was writing his dissertation on Steinbeck. How could he have left her? She must have turned heads wherever she went, whether to the hairdresser or a public lecture on campus. She invited Deborah and me to her house a few times. We knew Betty's side of the story, how she typed his term papers and poems and short stories, laundered his clothes and raised his children, the issue of what she had assumed was a permanent, unassailable union. Their children are grown now, married with kids of their own, and were always closer to Betty than to their father, who until he died taught one graduate seminar a year and traveled the world researching the subject of his next book, accompanied by his new wife and assistant, one and the same, a capable young woman his daughter's age who edited the university's literary magazine.

Betty would have consumed a goodly measure of red wine by the time she got talking about her ex-husband. We knew by the time her bitterness had filled the room and begun to smell acrid that our exit was only minutes away. We would make a joke, usually about having to call a cab and wondering whether or not one would come that late in the evening and doubting it aloud, given our proximity to the notorious address only a few steps away from the DMZ of Betty's gravel driveway, and we'd begin the slow leave-taking, replete with thanks, tidbits of news that hadn't yet been told, while we stood in her entranceway, always the last to go because we felt both responsible for her and also the least familiar of her acquaintances, if that makes any sense, as if the emotional distance and physical proximity between our neighbour and us allowed Deborah and me to act in a custodial way.

Betty knew some poets and writers in town, all successful, all represented by busy, vigorous agents, and so she thought, wouldn't it be a great idea if we gathered at her house one evening for a literary salon. It was the kind of thing she used to do when she and Bernard were living in Princeton, and people like Joyce Carol Oates and her husband Raymond would drop by. I knew some of the other writers who attended Betty's party that evening and I can say truthfully that I felt almost no jealousy in response to their success. I was relaxed, funny and lucid, able to engage in the flow of ideas, the shifting rhythms of conversation. I had reviewed one of their books, favourably, I'm thankful in saying, since I didn't know the author very well and had thought her retiring to the point of distraction, that is, unable to be at ease in any group, a perception she repudiated that evening when she stood and recited an entire two-page poem by one of her good friends, also in attendance and recently short-listed for a national award.

It was the miraculous sort of evening that required no warm-up. We all arrived within fifteen minutes of each other and were immediately kind, as if we were recent graduates of the same addiction-treatment program. You'd have thought us best friends, that we had each other's back and thought fondly of each other's accomplishment no matter how slight or distant in memory.

Deborah did not enjoy such gatherings. She said she always felt square and poorly read among artists. I've never been able to alleviate her discomfort or her misperception in that regard. That night she begged off, happy to stay home and watch TV. She joked that she was going to call up a dirty video and drink mint julep, a beverage she has never consumed and never will, given her aversion to all things minty. Nevertheless, the evocation of the drink fit her impersonation of Scarlett O'Hara, like whom she tried to sound whenever she wanted me to feel guilty about doing anything without her. I said, "Frankly, my dear, I don't build a dam," kissed her, toted my gift-bottle of wine, skipped down the front steps and began the long walk across the street to Betty's.

I settled on a large ornate couch that had a velour nap the color of cranberry, and I was careful to the point of paralysis not to drop crumbs on it or let my wine spill. When Betty saw me sitting uncomfortably stiff she admonished me for it, making a show of interrupting all conversation to point out the various stains that had accrued over the years to mar the surface of the piece, which looked as if it belonged in a brothel or a museum.

"That one, there, move your leg, your other one. See that? I've tried everything. You'll never guess what that is, not if you stay here all night. That, my fine fellow, is blood, and not just one person's. Two. You're going to think I run some kind of horror house when I tell you whose. That, believe it or not, folks, is Bernie's O-Neg, mixed with another's. Now I should let you try to guess who. It would make such a terrific exercise: uncover the story, jack up the suspense. Well?" She lifted her chin and surveyed the room. "No takers? Nobody going to steal my thunder? And you call yourselves poets. Very well, then."

"Tuck in, everyone," said an old friend of Betty's who taught ESL and edited children's books. "Get comfy, fill your glasses." Betty laughed loudest. The evening, like a pattern of swirling, shifting eddies, was coalescing on her, its hostess, a woman who appeared in the focal light of an adoring gaiety to be someone who could have done anything she chose in life.

"My husband," she began, elongating the first two syllables of the phrase with such a comic emphasis that laughter again rose to a crescendo and dissipated like the aural equivalent of a child's Halloween sparkler, "as you know, was and still is a devoted—"

"Leafs fan!"

"—instructor. Behave yourself now. Scholarship—remember scholarship? Research. Publication. These were ever his necessaries, but they were insufficient without ... now what's the word?"

"Drink," came a droll male voice, that of a young man who had been one of Camphor's graduate students before being hired to teach English in the same department. Now that he enjoyed tenure he was free to express his preference, which in this case happened to be decidedly Betty over Bernie.

"Yes, there was undoubtedly that. I was going to say that my husband needed student contact almost more than he did accolades or grant money or, God forbid, time with his family. He is a born teacher, none can fault him for that. He listens. His students adore him. It doesn't seem to matter how old he gets or how great the age gap between them, he always tries to understand them, their concerns, their colloquialisms, their relative preparedness or lack thereof for his class. He's demanding, often hard on them. You know that, Philip," and the young academic who had evoked the spectre of Professor Camphor's drinking nodded and blushed.

"We're into it, aren't we," Betty continued. "You'd think this was a wake, that the man was dead and we were trying to remember something good to say about him. This began as a joke and there's no way out but to tell it. Indelible stains on the sofa. This is what it all reduces to."

Seeing her reluctance to continue, two of the women, one after the other, urged her to let it go. She was under no obligation to dredge the murky reservoir of her past merely for our entertainment. We had diverted each other admirably for the past four hours and we were perceptive and diplomatic enough to call it a night. We were determined to leave smiling, all the while knowing that we had to get out of there before Betty fell into a tiger pit of her own making.

No one moved. I'd never seen a room full of people look so quickly restive, like a group of condemned prisoners searching shifty-eyed for the means of escape.

"You don't notice it unless you look closely. It looks like somebody spilled water. I'm always doing that, leaning over, forgetting the glass is in my hand. That velour—not the most practical of fabrics, but one thing it does well is act like an ever-loving sponge. Most spills sink in, go deep, to use one of Bernie's favourite phrases. Go deep, he would say to our son when they'd be throwing the football around out on the street after supper on one of those glorious summer days when the evening meal splits the day rather than brings it to a close. He went deep, he certainly did, with that little minx."

I'm a firm believer in intuition, that knowledge, seconds before it happens, that the phone is going to ring. We wake in the night for no apparent reason and can't fall back to sleep. In the morning we learn that a loved one has died, that she passed to the next realm the instant we awoke in darkness. Betty Camphor clamped her mouth shut before saying anything more. We squirmed where we sat, poised to leave but wanting to do it properly, to make it seem as if we had only that moment decided to go home. Preoccupied with this thought, I missed hearing the beginning of the commotion outside.

Two male voices were raised confrontationally one against the other and, despite the learnedness of one and the common ignorance of the other, were for the most part indistinguishable. The occasional word was distinct. A scuffle of gravel under foot, a barked curse, and then came the shudder of an impact transferred to us through the floor boards as something, a body presumably, collided with a structural and unforgiving portion of the front porch.

Deborah said she heard the noise from across the street and thought that I was one of the two figures she saw grappling outside Betty's. A second look with the birding binoculars corrected her misperception. That she could have thought me capable of such action makes me feel more exotic than brutish. We've been married over thirty years and in that time I have not physically fought another person. I assumed that my self-image was the same as the one she held of me, that of a contemplative, retiring, somewhat sensitive man who passes his day sitting archaically in front of a desktop manual typewriter. Knowing that I am not a scrapper and never will be takes nothing away from the fantasy, now ineradicable since my wife suggested it, of me as a man of pugilistic action, and I wondered whether or not she thought hopefully about me in that way. I have read that we never fully distance ourselves from our primitive instincts, and that women become aroused by a man's exhibition of physical prowess.

But it wasn't me she saw, it was Bernard Camphor rolling across the painted wood floor of his ex-wife's porch with the same fellow who had been using our address as a drop-box for his illicit social-insurance cheques. I was reluctant to go outside until Betty, peering through a gap in her drapes, assured us that it was Bernie out there, looking as if he were going to be murdered by a mugger.

He had arrived unaware that Betty was hosting a party, and when he saw her driveway filled with cars he decided to park in the front yard of the crack house next door. Or what used to be the crack house; since the day of the raid and arrests, no one had been living there, either in the upstairs apartment, most recently occupied by a man who worked at a nearby liquor store, or downstairs in the apartment where the flow of buyers had seemed unquenchable. Stewart Munce, welfare fraud, had been inside, trying a key that no longer worked, and he was angry when he emerged, at about the same moment Camphor was getting out of his car. Parallel tire tracks were worn there in the ground under a glorious copper maple that refused to be diminished by the uninspiring architecture of the building behind it.

The ensuing exchange is not difficult to imagine or to render believably:

"You can't park there, dude."

"Yes I can. I just did. My ability in the matter has been demonstrated."

"Smart guy, huh?"

"It's a relative measure. Set against the only standard present, I am brilliant."

"You got five seconds to move your car the fuck off my lawn."

"My good man, neither is this sorry patch of ground anything resembling lawn nor is it in any sense yours, unless you happen to be native American and are making an ancestral land claim, in which case you would be better armed with a treaty signed by one of my forebears instead of the sizable vacuum you appear to be carrying. Between your ears."

"What was that you said?"

"*Quod est demonstratum.* I said good night to you. I have business of a domestic nature here at your neighbour's. Or should I say former neighbour."

At which point the antagonist follows the renowned author (or is it that the street-savvy survivor follows the *agent provocateur*?) onto Betty's porch, where Bernard is standing poised to ring her bell. He says, the emaciated young man, denizen of dark alleys, the user, the one hooked on a chemical substance that makes reality palatable, "Move your motherfucking asshole of a sonofabitch car or lose it," with a chilly calm none could confuse with that of a kidder.

"What are you implying? That while I'm inside my wife's house—"

"Ex. She can't stand the sight of you. She told me."

"Did she indeed?"

"You calling me a liar?"

"Yes, I am doing precisely that. Throw in self-confessed thief. No argument with you in that regard."

I give Camphor the last word before the first punch is thrown, assuming that it was a punch and not a kick to the groin or a head-butt to the face. Furthermore I'm assuming that the professor was the recipient of the initiating blow. I admit my bias, however, prejudicial, in favour of those who contribute to society, who teach and are exceptional, whose work is valued, who write important books at a time when reading is derided, who prefer to fight verbally than with the hard, unforgiving parts of their bodies.

It fell to me, the only male guest remaining, to go outside to see what might be done to stop the combatants. The last sight I expected was Camphor seated on his opponent's back at about the shoulder blades and facing the addict's heels. Bernard was in possession of the fellow's feet and he was pulling on them, bending the toes towards him. It was the kind of torment I used to visit upon my younger brothers when we were children, usually after having watched professional wrestling on TV, and I barked a laugh that neither of them acknowledged. I expected to hear Camphor demand that ultimate expression of surrender, "Uncle."

"Feel that? You getting the full effect?"

"Yeah. Fuh. Uh-huhn. That's the ticket," said Stewart Munce in a voice muffled by his crossed forearms.

"You are paying for a sedentary lifestyle, my friend."

"I work out."

"Don't tell me. You press three-fifty."

"Three. I got a bike, too."

"Undoubtedly stolen."

"That's an unfair assumption. Oh shit! There. Yo."

"It's not the quantity of the exercise that's important, pal, but the quality. You've been working your muscles all in one direction. Try this."

He let the prone man's legs drop to the floor. "Now stay in this position. Relax a moment. Breathe deeply in and out a few times. Let the tension drain from your neck, shoulders, arms. Feel it pass down the length of your body like an electric current. That's the trapped energy you have to release. It's sitting there doing strange things to your muscles, joints, tendons, internal organs."

"You're the strange one."

"May I remind you that it was not I who moments ago was screaming in pain from charley horse and shin splints? The ultimate one-two, that. Now listen. With your hands just so, I want you to push down gently on the floor and at the same time lift your head slowly. Think of yourself as a cobra rising from a conjurer's wicker basket. Think about the vertebrae in your neck. As you bring your shoulders and head off the ground—don't strain; if it begins to hurt, ease off—imagine that you are increasing the space between each section of your spine. Think of yourself as a living accordion."

"My hamstr—starting to—hurts! Crapshitmotherfuhcocksuckohgaw!"

Camphor was able to address the man's immediate pain by rolling him onto his back, lifting the problem leg, resting it on his, Bernard's, shoulder, and bending the foot, toes towards the shin, to stretch the quadriceps. Stewart's face unclenched.

"You're not eating properly, that much is clear."

"What do you mean, *properly?*"

"Anything not beige, not processed, not deep-fried, not served in a plastic container."

"You're telling me what not to eat? You jump me like I'm a criminal, you sit on me, and now you're the food police?"

"I didn't jump you. I was defending myself. You put your hand on me."

"Yeah, well, you weren't listening."

"It's a de facto car park. All it's missing is a sign to that effect."

"Sure, drive anywhere, drive right over whoever's in your way. That's all you people ever do. You don't see what's under your noses and you don't listen."

"How does it feel now?" said Camphor, lowering the leg and rolling Stewart Munce once again onto his front. Straddling him and facing his head, he began to massage Munce's neck and shoulder muscles.

"Fine. You can let me up now." Under his breath he said, "Freakin' queer."

Munce rolled onto his side before pulling himself onto his knees and standing. For the first time since he had confronted Camphor, he saw me looking down at him, and Betty and her three remaining guests standing in the window. I suppose he was uncomfortable with an audience, because he hustled away up the street without making a final statement concerning the parked car, the loss of his shelter, the condition of his cramping leg or his inferior position in an unfair world.

I didn't see him again after that. I assume that Social Services caught up with him, cut off his income and alerted the police. I really don't know. I do know that before witnessing Bernard Camphor treat that man with a loving, healing touch, I was prepared to write Stewart Munce off as a lost cause, the by-product of an inequitable system or perhaps a cruel but efficient one that tested everyone's ability to cope. I think about him, his defensiveness, his prickly outrage and tacit acceptance of his place amidst life's brambles. No one was going to help him, he had to take care of himself. It must have been a shock to be attended to in that way by someone of Camphor's stature, the essence of which, if not the author and teacher's actual achievements, Stewart must have understood. Although I don't hold to any romantic notion that his having a charley horse treated by Bernard Camphor somehow turned Munce into an exemplary member of society, I wonder whether or not he ever passed the love up the bucket line, as my father the armchair philosopher used to say.

That such an absurdly comic tussle between the two men should end so soothingly in such a denouement of depleted ire and shy-making tenderness left me frankly off-balance for the rest of the night, during which I didn't sleep. Deborah awoke when I got into bed and I tried to tell her the story of what had happened, but she was too sleepy and had soon drifted off. I lay awake until after three, thinking about the entire architecture of the party, the various exchanges I'd had, the encounter between Munce and Camphor, even the reason why I enjoyed a tenuous relationship with each. I didn't get a chance to ask Camphor what it was about "Hot Yoga Above Diamonds" he found so funny. Perhaps it was the image of my main character, the young husband, overdressed and drenched in the purposefully high temperature and humidity of the workout room above the jewellery store, and surrounded by supple women, relaxed, well rested, good-looking women unencumbered by babies or sore breasts. Or was it that Betty misinterpreted his laughter as being critical rather than celebratory. An easy mistake, especially in a couple no longer together and harbouring resentment, disappointment and regret in varying measure.

Betty had blood stains on her divan because she had stabbed Bernard and the young woman he was trying to make love to at the time, in the house he and Betty were renting in Princeton. Perhaps "stab" is too dramatic a word. Both victims, according to the police report quoted in the news, received superficial cuts, a single slash each in the upper arm. The attack would probably not have been reported had an astute intern not become suspicious of the wounds, which Bernard was not able adequately to explain away while he and the young woman sat in different examination rooms, and of the placid older woman sitting in the waiting area, the bone handle of a carving knife sticking out of the top of her handbag.

I was finally drifting off when sirens sounded. In my hypnagogic state, I thought that the drug dealer and her associate, the man in American Civil War garb, were again being arrested. This time I didn't get out of bed to look out the window. As I fell asleep the red lights shone through the bedroom curtains, illuminating a dream I couldn't remember in the morning.

Betty used a different weapon that night after all her guests had left, two, in fact: long, sharp, stainless-steel skewers used for barbequing kabobs. This time she knew what she was doing. She wasn't trying to scare him, wasn't sending a desperate, angry message that was also a plea. The first attack, the one in Princeton, landed her a suspended sentence, given the situation and the nature of the wounds, shallow, almost ceremonial incisions into the fleshy part of the shoulder at the same spot on each of their arms. Then, the cuts required only a couple of butterfly closures to stop the bleeding. Betty underwent some psychiatric assessment and was determined to have been temporarily deranged in reaction to her husband's infidelity. This time, however, she didn't let anyone miss her intention. She slid one skewer through his neck from side to side as if he were a tender piece of lamb readied for the grill. The other she drove between two ribs from behind and into his heart. Being deep puncture wounds, they hardly bled externally. Betty Camphor was someone who learned from her mistakes.

I couldn't understand why she chose to do it then. They'd been estranged for years. They even seemed to have grown back into friendship, sharing a chuckle over a short story by a recently arrived neighbour. Deborah knew why. She knew without hesitation.

"You say she saw Bernard help that guy? She watched him do all that physio and yoga stuff to his leg? Think about it," she said.

"I have been."

"Camphor bestowed on a stranger, a scruffy junkie, the kind of intimacy you'd normally reserve for a spouse. It must have driven her out of her mind, especially if it was the kind of attention she never got from him. She still loved him. She was holding on to the impossible hope that he'd return to her."

"And give her deep massage."

"Yeah, well. Attention. That's the point. That's all I'm getting at."

We moved to a different part of the city three months later. It's a good area: low crime rate, good services and pleasant neighbours. Often we don't even lock our doors. We do attend, promptly, to each other's needs.

MR. GREENAWAY
RIGHTS THE WRONG

MR. GREENAWAY
RIGHTS THE WRONG

ONE YEAR, LATE in June, when Connie was in her early teens, her father hosted the end-of-school party for his colleagues. It was expected that each teacher would open his house for this purpose and Mr. Greenaway had not yet taken his turn. By nature he was not gregarious. He loved teaching, and his students adored him, most of them exceeding their expectations for achievement in the subject, but he was a private man who cherished his time at home. Although he would open his arms wide to any student in need, his fellow teachers knew him to be a reserved sort, unfashionable in attire and speech, unlikely to be found relaxing in the staff room. And so perhaps those most surprised to hear that he was hosting the staff "June is Busting Out All Over" bash were his peers.

It took place on a Friday. The students had been on vacation for a week, allowing their teachers to clean up their files, meet to talk about issues not dealt with during the year, review their courses, and bask in a feeling of relative ease. They drifted in and out of the staff room and each other's classrooms, talking about the year, particular triumphs, failures, personalities, approaches they thought they might try in September, leaves of absence they were finally brave enough to take, and doubts about their ability to continue teaching until retirement. Sometimes, in confidence, they revealed intimacies no one else had ever heard. This was the time of year when defences dropped away. A man in his early forties might confess his attraction for one of his students, startling his best friend, who quickly loses his clown-like grin when he sees that his pal is serious, that regardless of whether or not the man acted upon his infatuation he is as close to committing a grave error as he will ever be again. Or, perhaps with the giddy lightening air of someone doffing her chains, a woman tells her confessor that she will soon be leaving her husband and that, requited or not, she feels she must express her desire for this woman, her present audience. For, Connie remembered her father saying, another unforgettable, strike-me-dead instance of someone stepping outside his palisade, it was impossible to spend so much time with so many vital young people and not feel one's oats. Speaking at that time not of himself but a colleague, a man who had gone so far as to marry one of his students while she was still taking his class, Connie's father was, unbelievably, defending the man. The age difference, fifteen years, between the newlyweds, her father pointed out, was the same span separating his own maternal grandparents. "They were married almost sixty years," he said, "and he survived her."

He gave Connie and her mother a month's warning of the staff party, telling them with a nervousness he did not even try to hide that he would handle all the arrangements. They did not have a swimming pool, a minor deduction in social points. Still, they were not a city vying to host the Olympic Games. The party required a venue, and their house, like it or not, was it. The weather had been hot the past week. A swimming pool certainly would have been nice, thought Connie, thinking not at all about the gathering to come. Neither was the house equipped with air conditioning.

"I'll have to have plenty of ice on hand, buckets full."

Her mother shook her head doubtfully, knowing that she would be the one to get the ice, the buckets, and pretty well everything else her husband would need to make his event a success.

The one thing he did do was to hire a catering company to provide the food. Connie's mother blanched when she saw the bill. "You're going to have to give something up," she told him. He had already renewed his membership at his golf course and balked at the suggestion that he quit mid-season and get a refund. It was not something one did, he argued. The club looked unkindly on such behaviour.

"Such behaviour!" exclaimed his wife in an innocent foreshadowing of events to come. "You're giving something up, that's all there is to it."

Connie could not remember what her father sacrificed to pay for the party, or if indeed he gave anything up. It happened. It was paid for. Items were repaired or replaced. She still got to go away to camp in July.

The plan was that Connie, her best friend Debbie Mueller, and the girls' mothers would take the afternoon of the party off to shop for summer clothes. They drove to a mall in the west end, where they ate lunch, drifted through the stores, stopped mid-afternoon for tea, and in the interim found everything they were looking for and more. Connie's mother wore an expression Connie had never noticed before, one that said, along with her uncharacteristically giddy, nervous demeanour, "Let him have his fun. We can, too!" She wasn't going to let that man spend them into poverty all on his own. When Connie warmed to a style of dress, her mother nudged her towards a more expensive label, and where one item sufficed, she bought two.

At lunch the mothers ordered white wine. When it arrived Connie's mother said to the flustered waitress, "Did you have to run out and buy it? That's all right, dear. At least you have burgers. Mmm, my favourite."

Debbie's mother laughed loudly at this as if it were the funniest joke in the world. The restaurant was one franchise in a chain, conveniently located in the mall and designed to cater to the tastes of people Connie and Debbie's age. It was more than likely that someone in the kitchen *had* run out the back door and down the service corridor to the liquor store to find the requested label and vintage.

The arrangement they made with her father was that they would stay away until ten o'clock that evening. It seemed to provide ample time for a party starting at ten in the morning to exhaust itself. And so in keeping with the plan, they drove from the mall to an aquatics centre that had a giant water slide, a wave simulator, whirlpools, hot-tubs and a tinted-glass-enclosed area. The mothers soaked in the hot tub while the daughters, shrieking crazily, goaded each other to try the more daring of the amusements. They climbed three stories to the ceiling of the complex, where they crawled into plastic tubing through which they slid in a stream of water to drop, splashing, into an agitated pool. They swung Tarzan-style from suspended ropes into pretend lagoons. They let strong waves toss them onto an imaginary beach. Their mothers, yawning in the damp sapping heat, spoke in lazy intimate tones. Connie was too busy being a semi-savage to wonder what the women were talking about. Now, thinking back to that day, she tried to eavesdrop. Her mother had not said a word, at lunch or while they shopped, about the party, which was by now going full-tilt in her home. Perhaps while she lolled in the soothing water, her hair held up off the back of her neck and shoulders with a kerchief, she spoke her misgivings. But that wasn't what the expression on her face had indicated. Was Constance providing that detail now after decades had passed, filling in either what memory had failed to retain or what had never registered? I am there as my mother: what do I talk about?

Connie had been friends with Debbie since kindergarten and their mothers had become automatic friends in that way that young mothers did then. They made their houses and children their profession. Debbie had three brothers and a sister, surrogate siblings for Connie. The home, the community, the education of young citizens—these were their concerns, these filled their days. What would two such women, well known and appreciated as volunteers in the school, PTA members, freed from their schedules for one long luxuriant afternoon and evening, talk about? What intimacies did they unwrap for each other?

After the swim they drove downtown, parked in an underground lot in a building that housed a movie complex, and watched *American Graffiti*, twice, gorging on popcorn, soft drinks and candy, finally stumbling out into the dusk of one of the longest days of the year and, feeling hungry, ill, bloated, stiff, happy, disoriented, guilty, carefree, childish and wise, searched for the car. In the girls' estimation it was the best film ever made. Over the course of the summer they managed to see it four more times.

It was ten to ten. Like the characters in the movie, the ones played by Ron Howard and Richard Dreyfus, Connie did not want the night to end. She dreamed that she was one of them, that she stood poised on the brink of some new chapter in her life, but that she still had time.

"Perfect timing," said her mother, a note of trepidation in her voice. She was anxious to get home. She had no idea what to expect. They drove Debbie and her mother to their house, lingered over good-byes just long enough that the fullness of the day might be savoured and not immediately relinquished, and then got back into the car and drove home.

It had been her mother's sanctuary, that house, a two-storey white colonial with understated square columns, four of them, unadorned, supporting an overhanging porch-roof that ran the width of the building. The trim and shutters were hunter green. Her father had turned the original carport into an enclosed garage with a bedroom over it. The house got a fresh coat of paint every four years. Her mother had done all the landscaping and had kept the evergreen shrubs trimmed, fed, watered and covered with burlap and A-frame boards in winter. She had been the one to cut the grass. She said she was afraid her husband was going to run over the cord and electrocute himself. Connie knew that he was more than competent enough to handle the electric lawn mower. And grass was grass, to her eyes, when she had been a girl and now. It didn't matter who was pushing the machine, the result was more or less the same. No, her theory was that without the suggestion that the house and grounds would crumble to dust and wither to straw without her labour, her mother had nothing and nowhere to hide her guilt. This was her contribution. It was the way she paid for her room and board. *Am I imagining this?* Constance wondered. No, those were her words; her mother used to say such things as "kept woman" and "my humble contribution" and "earn my keep." *My humble contribution, what little it be.* Had these been bitter, ironic statements? What had she meant by them? Running back over all her mother used to do to manage the household made Constance feel entirely inadequate. *My God,* she thought, *she ironed everything! She pressed my underwear. She waxed and polished the floor. Every window was washed inside and out twice a year. Everything gleamed.* The cooking, too: baked desserts almost every supper. Guests at the table almost every night: Debbie, who said that she liked staying for supper with the Greenaways because her own house was chaotic by comparison; cousins; colleagues of her father; old high-school friends of her mother; single women; sometimes pairs of single women her father referred to as spinsters. The memorable fact was that her mother was rarely at rest, which made her humble, self-diminishing remarks disingenuous. No, she did not bring in a salary, though she did have a small legacy of stocks left her by her mother, but often she was still at work, sewing, knitting, mending clothes, painting trim, cooking for the week ahead, ironing the laundered clothes, when Connie and her father kissed her good night. What secret longing, what resentment if any, did she communicate to Debbie's mother that indulgent afternoon in the soothing water? It had to be about the unlived life, thought Constance. If her mother had not, during those un- guarded moments of languor and lotus eating, unloaded her heart, the alternative in all its nullifying banality was too terrible to contemplate.

All the lights were off and no music played. A fog of cigarette smoke hung in every room Connie and her mother passed through. From the back yard came low murmurs and through the dining room window they saw the red glowing buttons intensify when a smoker inhaled and the quick flare of a match or lighter. This appeared to be a stalwart cadre of seven or eight hangers-on. None was drinking: the alcohol had run out around nine, her father informed them the next day. It was the first and only time she saw her father drunk. He was sitting on an empty metal beer keg that lay on its side, straddling it and leaning forward on his hands to steady himself. The others were sitting or standing in a ragged circle around him, and it became clear that this silence that the moviegoers had returned to was a pause in the story he had been telling. A man took a deep hissing drag on a cigarette, but he didn't hold it the way Connie's parents held theirs when they smoked, and they never shared with anyone else. The roach was passed from a woman to a man, who inhaled before holding it out, breath held, at arm's length to the host. Connie's father did not respond to the offer and it went to someone else. His head hung low, almost to the surface of the keg, and he looked to be asleep. The window was open and they heard everything he said when his head did pop up.

The story was one Connie had not heard before, and from the way her mother remained at frozen attention it was one she did not know either. So intent was she on hearing what her father said that Connie did not notice what would be painfully obvious when the lights went on in the house: overflowing ashtrays, saucers, cups and bowls full of butts and food scraps, dirty wine glasses, some with lipstick smears near the rim, some with dead cigarettes floating in the dregs. Beer bottles and cans littered the counter and floor. Spills of red wine looked like blood spots on the pale shag carpet in the living room. Burn marks marred the surface of the dining room table, her mother's lemon-oiled teak treasure. The cushions of the sofa were askew and, though they could be easily righted, one was ripped as if a razor had been applied to it. A curtain hung crookedly: on closer inspection they found that three of its hooks had come away from the fabric and were still attached to the eyelets in the runner. The broken pieces of a crystal highball glass were in a pile on the tile hearth of the fireplace, as if someone had begun to sweep them up and become distracted. Mosquitoes moved in and out of an unscreened window that had served as the takeout portal for drinks.

The party had begun sedately, orderly enough in the late morning, with teachers (These are teachers! Connie at one point was startled to realize) arranged on folding chairs in the shade, paper plates of food balanced on their knees. Her father had borrowed a gas barbeque from a neighbour and, to supplement the catered dishes, he insisted on cooking superfluous hamburgers and hotdogs although, as far as Connie knew, he had never done such a thing in his life. He had been solicitous enough to alert the neighbours on each side and behind them that they might hear some merriment that afternoon and evening. It would be wrapped up by ten, they had his word on it. Of course, he added, they were invited, and people from two of the three households had made an appearance. To be on bad terms with one's neighbours was an intolerable notion to Mr. Greenaway. A Jack Russell terrier they used to have when Connie was a little girl had to be gotten rid of when it merely snapped at a toddler who had wandered into the yard from next door.

The party might well have remained outdoors had a brief but violent thunderstorm, one Connie and her mother had missed while they watched the movie, not made them scatter for cover. The storm cooled the air. Lights snapped on inside the house. Guests made themselves comfortable. Fresh drinks were poured. The conversations grew louder, bolder, more ribald. The old storytellers held sway. Some of the younger women found music they could dance to. Athletes descended to the basement, where they found games of darts and table tennis. A man carrying a few extra pounds was demonstrating his overhead smash, a move that required he lift his body off the floor using his free hand for leverage on the playing surface, when he collapsed the table, its aluminium legs having buckled, leading his opponent to attempt the same on his side. The result was prolonged sprawled hilarity, the game continuing with the men lying down. The light outside dropped, lamps inside were switched off, the rain evaporated and the temperature climbed. Couples stole to the bedrooms and reappeared some time later, soon enough not to have been missed. The sensible ones drifted home before this stage, the one marked by darkness and the smell of burning rope and the blare of music played too loudly. A neighbour, the one who had provided the barbeque and who had been at the party earlier, returned to ask them to turn down the stereo, and they did so, apologizing. The hard core went outside. Connie's father smoked his first joint and then his second and began to tell a story about the death of his best friend, a story he struggled to finish.

They had skipped school to swim in the St. John River. His friend dived from a high bluff into what he had thought was a deep pool, but he was mistaken and broke his neck. Connie's father climbed down after he heard the awful sound. The boy's body was carried quickly downstream and was not recovered until the next day. They were ten years old.

As Connie's father sat straddling the beer keg in his back yard like a gentleman cowboy astride a silver bull, preparing for the gate to open and the ride of his life to begin, he lifted his head to continue the story. He had known that that spot, the bluff, was not the right place. The deep pool was another two hundred yards upstream. The other boy was someone he admired more than liked, though they called each other "best friend." The boy who had died had used his size to intimidate smaller children. Connie's father told his drunk, stoned audience that he had kept his mouth shut that day so long ago. The bully had called him a sissy for not wanting to dive first. I'll show you, said the domineering boy. I'll show the sissy how it's done.

"I could have warned him. I knew, you see. I knew it wasn't the safe spot. I was angry at him. He had been taunting me all day, daring me to skip school, teasing me for the way I spoke, dressed, ran, threw a ball, climbed trees. I don't know why I thought he was my best friend. I don't know why I kept going up the river with him."

The group was quiet a long time. A man coughed nervously and tried to read the time on his watch, bringing the face of it close to his eyes, tilting it this way and that to catch some of the ambient light. It was late, someone said, and the observation was repeated, covering the awkwardness of Connie's father's confession, pushing it aside. They patted their pockets for car keys, drained their glasses, and thanked their host. The words of appreciation were abbreviated and hurried, as if their speakers had awoken in a strange bed and had no idea how they got there. A man helped Connie's father off his beer-keg mount and waited until he saw that he could stand on his own. They moved to the side of the house, where they followed a flagstone path to the street and their parked cars.

"He mustn't see us here," said her mother. "Quick, up to bed," and Connie, uneasy about making her way upstairs in the dark, wanted even less to remain in the midst of the ugly scene with its evidence that adults could be childish, debauched, out of control.

LATE JULY, AFTER she returned from camp, she asked her father to tell her the whole story from the beginning.

"What story would that be?"

"The one about you and your friend at the river." She had to confess then that she and her mother had been inside the housing, listening, and that they had arrived while he was in the middle of telling the story. At first he was embarrassed and she thought he might become angry with her. She judiciously failed to mention that she knew he had been intoxicated and that he had looked silly straddling the barrel.

They were sitting at the edge of the beach, under the shade of a tall red pine. He was sitting in his favourite chair, a deeply canted Adirondack that supported his back. Across the arms of the chair he had placed a board on the surface of which he was arranging plastic geometric shapes, tessellation pieces he planned to introduce to his classes in the fall. With each completed design he sketched its rudiments on a thick pad of graph paper. Connie lay on a blanket near his feet. In from swimming, she had stretched out in the sun to dry off and had felt her skin beginning to burn.

He told her the complete story of the boy's death. A tone of wonder coloured his usual matter-of-fact delivery. None of the pathos of his revelation at the party remained. It had happened, the accident at the river, an unfortunate event. Connie wanted to ask him questions, but held her tongue. She wanted more of the beautiful raw sadness, the noble regret he had expressed in the dark. She wanted to experience what his audience had. Don't you feel guilty? she wanted to ask. Do you think he would be alive today if you had warned him? Why didn't you say something? She let herself wallow in the loss, the feeling of forever and never, the way she had hugged herself coming out of the movie into the warm muggy night air, trying to hold on to the delicate strands of *our last night together* and *gone* and *when we were young and in love.*

Perhaps our first awareness of complicity marks the true end of childhood. One might say that we cease being children when we see that our parents are not immortal or morally perfect, are neither geniuses nor omnipotent gods. But as she thought about that pivotal night, Constance understood that she had always known, even as a young child, what being human entailed. She was suspicious and always had been of claims of magic, listened with sceptical reserve to the fantastic details of fairy tales, hoped that Santa Claus was real but knew in her heart that he could not be. And so in a way she always thought of herself as being aware of the truth that hid behind perception. The white lies, the censored parts, the details conveniently left out. For her, childhood ended at that moment when she chose to take part in an act of omission, when she stopped herself from asking, "Why?" and "Why not?" and "How can you live with yourself knowing that you failed to act?" She had seen her father vulnerable and compromised, a fool confessor, his sanctuary raided and trashed, his barrel emptied. He was the least noble figure he could have been that night. On the beach, again enthroned, working through the elegant geometrical designs on his lap, he was her father once more, and this pretence of recovery, instead of making her indignant, angry, contemptuous of the duplicity of adults, made her want to do all she could to protect him.

The prospect of the month ahead, alone with her parents in the little cottage, made her happy to the verge of delirium. She was sad for the boy who had died, but that was in the past and people were always dying. He would have been an old man had he lived, mid-forties, her father's age, and might well have succumbed to an illness or another accident by now. She had found camp fun and tiring, and after the first week-long session, repetitive. The counsellors never gave them enough free time. It seemed that every minute was scheduled: sports, aquatics, arts and crafts, hikes, wood gathering and the nightly bonfire with its songs and predictable ghost stories. She was glad it was finally over, three camps in succession. This month, bittersweet plump August cradling the slowly dying ember of summer in its palm—she would embrace this time so tightly that it would defy consumption. She had her favourite books, her jigsaw puzzles, card games with Mum and Dad, whom she never thought of as being her best friends though they were. Best Friend was Debbie. She believed she would know Debbie, who was coming to spend the final week of summer with them, all her life. And yet who knew Connie better than her parents did? And who knew them better than she? Her father had survived a childhood trauma, and as such was elevated in her esteem. He had experienced the kind of life altering drama she could only dream about. Someday, she vowed, something like that would happen to her. And yet, as if to contradict his vital harrowing past, here her father was, with his skinny, hairless, varicose veined, white legs, his high furrowed brow, his crazy, kinky, thinning, grey hair, his unstylish, thick eyeglasses.

BECAUSE HE HAD promised to do so and because he wanted his daughter to see that being aware of a problem and doing something to alleviate it are two widely separate notions, Connie's father invited two poor Haitian brothers, younger than she, to spend a week with them at a cottage. Much to her displeasure, her father erected a tent for the boys in a little clearing just up from the high-water line of the beach. It was a grassy square, protected on three sides by trees and bushes, where Connie liked to lie in a hammock and read. The brothers seemed dangerous to her in their strange, sometimes wild behaviour. They were given Ritalin to keep them orderly in school. Out at the lake, her father had contended, the boys didn't need any of that. Sun, water, trees, fresh air, hiking trails, boats, bonfires, sporting competitions—what more did they need?

Certainly not drugs. They would sleep like babies every night, he promised. "Sure," quipped her mother. "They'll wake up every two hours crying."

The elder of the two, Xavier, who had been in her father's class that year, took to the water as if he were an amphibious creature. They practically had to haul him out to get him to sit for meals. He and the dog, a hunting retriever, were always wet, all day. Not until after dark would Xavier, huddled under a wool blanket on the beach sand and staring intently at the fire, come close to being still. The dog kept close to the boy all week. Xavier had infinite patience, it seemed, for the animal's obsessive interest in the game of throw-and-retrieve. Anything the boy tossed into the water, a stick or a pine cone or a rock, the dog fetched, often after a remarkable time submerged.

Pedro spent his time either crying to go home or yelling at his big brother, who coped best by ignoring him. Once Connie saw Pedro bean him in the back of the head with an egg-sized rock, just after Xavier had sent a rubber ball into the lake for the dog. The resulting wound gushed, seemingly unstoppably, and her father drove the boy into the city to have the cut stitched closed. It had been a sickening and fascinating sight for Connie, who had not thought it possible, except on television, for someone to inflict such damage on another. When they returned, her father put Pedro back on his medication and the little boy spent much of the rest of his time there cocooned, like the filling of a sausage roll, in a towel on the beach.

Connie regarded Xavier as someone who had been heroically wounded, and became solicitous of him, bringing him glasses of pop in the hot sun—she with her fair hair and skin considered it to be scorching hot—and aspirin when he said that his head ached. He would not stay out of the water, even on a cold rainy day, and so Connie's mother made him wear one of her pink rubber bathing caps, which he did without being self-conscious about it. Connie watched him from where she lay on the sand and tried to sunbathe. It wasn't fair, she thought, that he should have such creamy smooth brown skin without having to work at it. At least her acne had subsided in the strong sunshine. Burned red, she resorted to covering her body in a blanket the way inert Pedro did.

At night, as she lay uncomfortably on a thin mattress spread over a steel folding cot with unforgiving springs, listening to her parents murmur and whisper before falling asleep, she pictured Xavier in the little red bathing suit her father had bought for him. Though only twelve, the boy was already developing the musculature of a man twice his age, the wide shoulders and deep chest tapering through taut abdominals to compact slim hips and buttocks. She thought that if Pedro were not there, too, she might sneak out to the tent. To do what? The particulars were not anything she could put into words then. She had tried erotic kissing only once, with an equally curious and inexperienced Debbie, and that had ended in embarrassed laughter. It was only gravity acting upon her. She was three years older than he. This wasn't the way it was supposed to be happening. She was supposed to get noticed by an older boy who then asked her to a dance, and it—love—would be established only when everybody saw them together.

The day her father prepared to drive Xavier and Pedro back to the city, Pedro cried, surprising everyone, and ran to hug Connie's mother, who had made a soft place in her heart for the sad little tyke. As always, Xavier's eyes were restless, never settling anywhere for more than a second or two. "One more swim," he said, but in his detached flat tone that spoke of an absent spirit. He accepted his teacher's command that he get into the car, now, please, without a fight. Connie felt immediate relief as she watched them drive off, and then began to dismantle the tent.

"Why don't you leave it up?" said her mother. "You might like to sleep out here."

"No," said Connie, "I'm going to put the hammock back up," but after the tent was stowed in its cylindrical canvas bag, she left the hammock where it was, folded under the front of the cottage.

It didn't occur to her until she was back at school that her father had brought the Haitian brothers to stay with them at the cottage because he felt guilty about that other boy's death so long ago. But that was exactly what he had been doing, she was sure of it. He had it in his mind to give those kids a few days in paradise: sun, sand, water, sailing, and not a care in the world. A Boys' Own Holiday. He must, being the father of an only daughter, have longed for a son, she also believed, though she had never heard him express such a regret. The tragedy of the boy's death had robbed him of his own happy, carefree, irresponsible, oblivious boyhood, and he would right that wrong somehow by doing this.

And, in doing so, steal a precious week of blissful vacation from said daughter.

How melodramatic, she thought. You weren't robbed of anything except a week of boredom. Face it, Constance, you enjoyed having that boy around. Tight perfect little bum, sleek hairless legs. You thought about him, yes you did, night and day. Especially at night under your covers. She was glad she had never told her father how angry she had been at him for inviting them, because now, missing him, thinking she would give anything to see him again, hear his baritone, find him asleep in his chair, gently lift his reading glasses off his face, where they sat slipped and askew, the thought of doing anything to spoil his memory was unthinkable.

THE YOUNG IN
THEIR COUNTRY

THE YOUNG
IN THEIR COUNTRY

△

THE EPISODE PEOPLE refer to when they talk about me, the unfortunate event they think led to my early retirement from teaching, was actually my attempt to illustrate an historical point. You see, most are not the passionate students of history that I am. How could they know that what the girl, one of my students, was yelling from inside the confines of her chosen cell was the most important utterance in the development of this country? I repeated the words, or a variation of them more pertinent to my situation, to my principal during my exit interview. She said I was lucky not to be in jail.

I knew that my time in the classroom was quickly drawing to a close the day after the incident in the school parking lot. The decisive moment came on a morning that began little differently from countless preceding it. I was standing in the staffroom, speaking to Eldon Grimshaw, biology and general science, when I suddenly knew that he could see what I looked like under my clothes. Rather than being upset by this, I found I enjoyed his discomfort at seeing me naked and being unable to say or do anything about it. I asked him whether or not he was feeling all right and, mischievously, I admit, told him that he looked ill. You would think that being exposed in this way and being unable to respond, I would be embarrassed, even demoralized, but such was not the case. In fact it was liberating. I looked around, wondering who else in the room could see me uncovered. Only Eldon had the equivalent of a comic-book hero's X-ray vision.

It became clear that day that only teachers, like Grimshaw, who thought that I did not deserve to be teaching at the school, a prestigious, liberal-arts-oriented high school, and those students who were failing my class, could see me in this unique way. Unlike their instructors, those students endowed with super-visual power succumbed to unregulated giggling. They were, after all, the ones who had no discipline and were naïve enough to assume that everyone's perception was the same as their own. I could not without exposing the ignorant in the class to the delicate nature of the problem—I was the only person whom the negatively elect could see naked—ask them what it was they were snickering at. But not to respond would have put me in an even trickier position, that of an instructor who had lost control of his class. Even the most conscientious among them, like sharks drawn to bloodied water, would want to see me brought low for my weakness.

One of my best students, Julie McAfee, a precocious girl two years younger than her peers, raised her hand. "Did I miss something?" she said. She was the type who would rather forgo a meal than not be privy to that which others knew. I suppose I had a crush on her, in that way in which teachers are allowed to fuss over their star pupils, not that this in any way excuses what I convinced her to do. I am trying, simply and objectively, to present the salient facts. She had dark-blond hair, steely blue eyes flecked with copper, a slim figure, and an insouciant athletic grace she tried to hide with a slouching posture. Julie McAfee may not have been the most intelligent person I ever taught, but she was among the two or three hardest working. I have been in the presence of pure raw intelligence only once or twice in my classroom, each time observed in someone for whom I would otherwise have no patience were I to meet him on the street. I refer to a species of antisocial lout who reveals little about himself other than an abiding disdain for the requirements of scholarship. My students and the younger of my colleagues did not hide the gentle derision they reserved for what they thought of as my hopelessly outdated views about education, particularly my use of such terms as "scholar," "knowledge," "achievement," and "rigour." These have long since the days of my formal training been replaced by terminology that better reflects the reality and needs of the "learner stakeholder," to quote a recent missive from the minister of education. I won't play coy. No one has less respect for the present administration than I. These bureaucratic narcoleptics have no idea what a student should or should not be getting from a publicly funded education.

The difference between, "Sir, you're naked," and "Oh my god, I can see his willy," used to be the difference between public and private discourse in this country. So much of what used to be clearly delineated is now blurred. Is it possible that there no longer exists such a thing as a private, unvoiced thought? You, sir, are naked, whether or not anyone else can see you, and it's my right to declare it, to post it on my web log, and there is nothing you can do about it.

I waited until the snickering had ended before making some concluding remarks about the unit we had been studying, "Rebellion and Justice in Post-Confederation Canada." They were nervous and excited, in anticipation of their dramatization of the trial of Louis Riel, which was to begin that period. One of them, Matthew Langara, raised his hand. Matt oscillated between diligence and sloth, such that he could occupy both camps repeatedly in the same fifty-minute period. This day he was content to be one of the keeners. He asked if we might carry out one of the executions, Thomas Scott's or Riel's, after the trial. Almost as one the class concurred.

Perhaps they had only that moment felt the power of their participation and seen that the outcome of the story depended upon their performance and the verdict. I think they wanted Riel to be found guilty so that they could re-enact his hanging. Whether it was the novelty of capital punishment, or that so many of them were already consumers of violent media, that made them so interested in that aspect of the story, I can't say for sure. I wanted to believe that whatever the outcome, in their hearts they would always side with the Riel and the Métis' doomed crusade for self-determination.

I told them I thought we had ahead of us more than enough drama for one week and the snickering flared again. "You might find him not guilty." I suggested that there might be an opportunity for the class to do some follow-up creative writing for extra credit. In their mock trial, much of the case against Riel was going to hinge upon the death of Thomas

Scott. "Take a side," I said. "You could write about the trial of Thomas Scott, presided over by that dastardly outlaw, Ambroise-Dydime Lépine, Riel's lieutenant. Or you could call it the execution of the troublesome Orangeman Scott by the heroic president of the provisional government at Fort Garry. Use your imaginations." They groaned. All they wanted was to perform a realistic execution. In their parlance it would be "way sick." In three decades of classroom teaching I have seen no discernible difference between the motivations of teenagers in the 1970s and their counterparts in the 2000s. Essentially they stand outside of history, regally unperturbed by anything beyond their immediate desires. That is, of course, until the moment they arrive at school in possession of extraordinary powers of sight.

Which is worse, I ask you: that imbeciles, ignorant of the lessons of history, occupy the offices of power or that your son can suddenly see that the circumference of his teacher's waist exceeds that of the pedant's chest, and that what used to be enviable pectoral muscles are now fleshy suggestions of a woman's breasts? Well, you reply, when you put it that way. When I put it that way, giving you a choice of extremes that have as much in common as do a swan and a cockroach, I can justify anything, can't I, lessening the sting of any lash to conscience. If there was one thing I wanted to teach these children, it was that they must first prepare the ground before embarking on any inquiry. The terms of the question must coexist. Faulty logic has no place in a just society, of which truth is the basis.

At this point, held to my own standard, I must confess two things. First, a private thought that may nevertheless have led to my bizarre exposure in the classroom that day: I enjoy the attention of women. Despite my expanding girth and slackening muscle tone, I believe that I have held on to my "looks." My second revelation is that a mentally unbalanced youth attacked me some six years ago, stabbing me with a sharp knife, superficially in the neck and upper back and deeper in the right thigh and abdomen. I was opening the door to my car in the school parking lot one afternoon when it happened. He was not someone I taught or even recognized, although he was a student at the school. Had I not been there then he would most certainly have maimed or killed someone else. My recovery and rehabilitation were slow and painful. I became addicted to strong painkillers. I still drink more hard liquor than is healthy for my liver. My wife, to whom I was married for two happy decades, can in no way be faulted for separating from me, after waiting, patiently, forbearingly, for me to heal. My body healed, eventually, one collapsed lung re-inflating, the muscles in my leg knitting, leaving me with a slight limp. We stay in touch through our son and three daughters, four adults now with busy lives of their own. The consensus is that I am better off living alone.

From time to time, as a speculative exercise meant only to prevent boredom and bolster my confidence, I would try to gauge my physical attractiveness to certain young women, always students in the senior grades and those who tended to be older and more mature in their attitudes and deportment than their peers. Of course I had no way of verifying my "readings," which were based on the most incidental of observations—a response to a joke, a blush after a compliment, a brief glance when the subject thought I wasn't looking—and I never acted upon what I perceived to be mutual interest. The point of this confession is to posit a question. Was I the agent of my undoing? By thinking that these girls, some younger than my youngest daughter is now, could be attracted to me, did I leave myself vulnerable to a kind of mystical retaliation, the exposure of my nakedness, a punishment I could not reveal for fear of being ridiculed, censured or reprimanded?

After the trial, in which history was vindicated and Riel found guilty, the verdict strongly influenced by Julie's work for the prosecution, the class wanted to talk more about the Scott affair. It was as if the courtroom battle had whetted their appetite for a truth that remained just beyond their reach. They gave up asking me to let them stage the hanging; only one ugly truth about human nature would that reveal. And so again we weighed the contradictory evidence surrounding Thomas Scott's death. He was shot by firing squad on March 4, 1870, having been stood up against the walls of Upper Fort Garry. Sectarian hot-head, abusive and difficult prisoner who might otherwise have lived had he kept his mouth shut, he had already escaped custody once. Why did he return? He apparently hated the French Catholic Métis that much. Once a troublemaker, always one? We even discussed the possibility that the firing squad had loaded their rifles with powder and wadding, but had neglected to include bullets, a far-fetched theory but one that seemed to support an associated one, that Scott was killed by a bystander named William O'Donoghue, who wanted the Orangeman dead, would not content himself with a mock execution, and who supposedly fired his pistol at the prisoner simultaneously with the rifle squad. He would have had to fire two quick shots, given that Scott was hit twice, once in the left shoulder and once in the chest, neither wound fatal. Another man then stepped forward and shot Scott in the head, but that too was a superficial wound, to the face. They put the bleeding man in a coffin-like container, from the confines of which he could be heard screaming, begging for release—freedom or merciful death—an entire day before he succumbed to blood loss, hypothermia or both.

I had the distinct feeling, for the few seconds following my communication of Scott's pathetic last words, which they all knew from the trial but appeared to be hearing for the first time, that everyone in the class could now see my shrivelled, lopsided testicles. The awareness, mine and theirs, lasted but a moment. Even Julie McAfee saw. She covered her uneasiness by raising her hand. "They left him in there to die. It's barbaric," the silver bullet of her argument. The way she said it, she could well have been accusing me.

"Well," I said, for the benefit of the others (Julie already knew this), "if it is true—and we have to remain sceptical, given the incendiary artwork and lurid journalism that English Canada consumed following the story—you can understand the outrage from the East. You had to decide and you did: if Thomas Scott had not been killed, and if these details, true or false, had not been attached to the account, would Louis Riel have been hanged?"

As they filed out the door at the end of the period, I wondered if they saw me as being anything but old, tedious and tolerably necessary to their success, whether or not I appeared before them dressed in my rumpled corduroy jacket and jeans or unclad. I would never know, being someone who would rather walk barefoot over broken glass than broach subjects of a personal nature with them. They knew that I had been knifed by a student years ago and they had heard about what had happened to Julie before the mock trial began. It was more than anyone needed to know about me. You can imagine how ludicrous would have been my asking them, then, 'By the way, before you go, how many of you this past week have been able to see past the barrier of my clothes? I'm merely curious. I mean, I'm aware that some of you can or did, and pretty sure that the lot of you got the full Monty there a few times. I'm asking for the purposes of my own research only. None of this will be taken down and used against you, you understand. You have the right to remain innocent as long as possible. Innocent: another morally relative term, one I reserve the right to continue to use, despite what you now know or suspect about the circumstances surrounding the death of one Thomas Scott, Northern Irish labourer, strike breaker, scrapper, nineteenth-century equivalent of today's neo-Nazi skinhead. Similarly you have the right to suffer silently the humiliation of knowing that I am not only human but grossly so, as evidenced by my far-from-ideal level of body fat. Think of the spare tire around my middle as an extra twenty bucks tucked away for emergencies. Emergency? That's what this moment is, your appalled faces say, you who are doomed to repeat history, those of you briefly blessed by revelation thanks to the tarnished martyr, T. Scott, and the few of you still blissfully in the dark. Not so blissfully, I suppose, now that I've described it in so many words.'

So many words, so few remembered. I can hardly distinguish one year of the past thirty from another. The content of what I taught rarely changed. The delivery may have swung like a pendulum according to the ruling pedagogy of the day, but the words themselves? I probably repeated the same sentence hundreds of times, and could if pressed reproduce the key points of any lesson in a form identical to the way I said them years ago. So what do my students remember? They remember the day I arrived to class with a big egg-stain on my tie, one decorated with a comic strip of Bugs Bunny and Daffy Duck discussing whether or not Porky Pig should have his citizenship revoked for the crime of gross indecency. The splattered bit of my rushed breakfast obliterated the punch line, which had Porky in the final frame saying, "B-b-b-but I thought you guys didn't mind a little wallowing between friends."

From the first day I arrived wearing the tie, this particular class had decided, out of a communal sense of fun, and accepting that I was friendly enough to let them do it, that they should read the entire strip aloud in unison. I liked them in return. As a group they had character and talent enough to make for an enjoyable year. But this day the word "wallowing" was a yolky blob with a double-u at one end and "ing" at the other. Out of habit they began the recitation, the laggards catching up with the others by the second frame, and when they arrived at the smudge most said the hidden word as they remembered it. It was a favourite necktie, after all, they enjoyed the bit of tomfoolery it always triggered, and I justified it thinking they might even go home and think about its message of tolerance. I wasn't going to kill the sweet potential of the moment by pulling out the hammer of didacticism and braining them with it. The oh-so-memorable catch in the routine came when my man Matt, the one who had wanted to stage a mock execution, someone who I hope is still his own person and has retained the strain of fresh anarchy and quirky humour that set him apart from the herd, replaced "wallowing" with "wanking." I had no choice but to laugh along with them—Matt made sure that his reedy voice rose above all others—and to accept the resultant jokes at my expense ("Are you sure it's egg yolk, sir?"), the inevitable ribbing about my eating habits.

The point of this digression is that I would bet easy money that every one of them, twelve or twenty years from now, will remember what Matt blurted out. The division of powers between the provinces and the federal governments at Confederation? I don't think so. The meaning of "Orangeman?" Maybe a few who follow the Irish situation. The origin of the term, "Bennett Buggy?" You would think that such an alliterative term would stick, but no. It gives one pause, doesn't it, calls into question the efficacy of all that curricular planning, all those classroom hours, because you can be sure that to this day they remember Matthew Langara's inspired though inappropriate word substitution. You can be equally assured that the sight of me naked is an indelible stain in their memories. Five who saw me in that way eventually failed the course. They populated the rearmost desks of the room. They picked their positions, not I; it was their choice to be distant, to eschew study, attention, application, attendance (though it was remarkable that those five were there all that revelatory week). And no, I'm sorry, I know what you're thinking, but I refuse to entertain the notion, the possibility that seeing me in the buff somehow stifled their ability to learn. Some got the credit at summer school and the rest returned to take the course again from another teacher in September. The point is that whatever they did, they never forgot what they saw. How could they?

Somewhere in this account is a lesson, but I'll be damned if I can flush it out. Those of my associates who considered me to be unworthy continued to do so until the day I resigned, although they never mentioned what they saw. People looked me in the eye or they looked out the window as they spoke, each according to his nature and his quirk. They fit their moulds and continued to deliver their predictable gifts. I wanted to test them to see whether or not they still possessed their extraordinary powers, since mine, the ability to see the world through their eyes, disappeared after that week of the trial. I suspected they were normal again, just as, following the incident involving Julie McAfee, they suspected that I had gone completely off my nut.

I had brought in some replicas of archival documents dealing with Riel, and the class had been spending a few periods poring over them in preparation for the staging of the trail. It left the history open to interpretation and the trial open to the possibility of a different outcome, given their assigned roles as members of the prosecution, defence, judiciary, legislature, etc. They had finished reading through the material, which was due back at the educational resource centre from which I'd borrowed it. Julie, as the chief barrister for the Crown, was still unclear about some of the evidence and wanted to talk to me about it. In particular she felt that the Thomas Scott affair was critical to her case, but had doubts about what had actually happened. If the intention had been merely to frighten Scott into submission by making him go through a mock execution, and if his death, if initially unintended, had been the result of misadventure followed by negligence, were these not to a certain degree extenuating circumstances?

I told her that she had to be careful. She was applying hindsight and a modern sensibility to the historical record. After all, in 1870 starving urchins were still being hanged for stealing loaves of bread. Riel was on trial for treason against the Crown.

"But Scott made things worse," she said. "He escaped from jail, came back, took part in an uprising, couldn't keep his mouth shut, insulting people and all that. He has to take some of the blame, don't you think?"

"Blame for his own death?"

"I don't know. Maybe? I don't think Riel should have been hanged because of it."

"He did lead a second rebellion, don't forget."

"I know, but everybody in English Canada was against him because of what happened to Thomas Scott. The way it got portrayed, it made Riel out to be a monster."

She helped me carry the boxes of papers out to my car and we kept talking about the case. I had never had a student so engaged by what she was learning. She wanted to be a lawyer, she said. She couldn't wait for the trial to begin. She wanted to anticipate everything the defence team was going to throw into her path.

We reached my car and I popped the trunk open using the remote button on my keychain. When she began to place her box inside, I stopped her. "You know," I said, "if you really want to be prepared for this trial, you have to know everything."

"What do you mean?"

"Well, what do you think it felt like for Thomas Scott to lie wounded and cold inside that wooden crate, his de facto coffin?"

"Pretty horrible."

"Yes, you can intellectualize it, but can you say you truly know?"

"Empathize, you mean?"

"Exactly."

A decisive look came over her. Without my having to say the words, she climbed into the trunk of my car, lay down on her side and pulled her knees to her chest, before I closed it on her. In a voice loud enough for her to hear I told her to imagine that she was the dying man, furious with his captors, outraged against all the powers, those of earth and heaven. I told her to yell at the top of her voice the words Thomas Scott was purported to have said: "For God's sake take me out of here or kill me!"

She did, repeatedly, louder each time at my urging. "Feel it," I said. "Feel his anger and his panic. He's an unrepentant racist, but does he deserve this? He knows he's going to die. This is the only way to sway a jury. You can talk facts at them until they fall asleep, but make this horror come alive and they are yours. The prisoner is bleeding. The shoulder and chest wounds have probably subsided, but the facial wound where your nose used to be gushes for a long time. You try to stop it with your hand, your sleeve, but the blood is clogging your air passages. It's lightless, bitter cold, still winter, you're abandoned, buried alive. Shivering uncontrollably. You relive the violations of your flesh, the first stab, the next and the next. Even if you were expecting them, the shock and pain are indescribable."

I didn't realize that she was crying, screaming to be let out, no longer acting, until one of my colleagues, Peter Baxter, ran across the lot, saw what was happening, pried my keys out of my hand and opened the trunk to let her out.

"What the hell is going on?" he demanded, pulling me to my feet. "How long was she in there?"

Eventually Julie was able to explain why I had locked her in the trunk of my car, and to her credit she told Baxter that she had been a willing participant. "I panicked," she said. "I guess I'm claustrophobic."

Baxter looked at her. He was sceptical, but he accepted her version of what had happened. He turned to me. "All right," he said, "that makes sense, sort of. But why were you crouched down, almost under the car? You had your arms up covering your head and neck."

"Did I?"

"Yes, you did."

"I suppose I got a little carried away with the re-enactment. Sorry."

"You're fine, then, both of you?"

We assured him we were. I could tell he was still suspicious. He filed a report with the principal, not that I blame him. I would have done the same. It hastened the inevitable, I suppose. I just wish he and others understood what Julie and I were trying to do. They don't see history the way we do.

ACKNOWLEDGEMENTS

▲

THE AUTHOR THANKS Maurice Mierau, Catharina de Bakker and Gregg Shilliday for giving this book a home, a face, a body and wheels. Thanks to Sharon Murphy, Valerie Compton and Steven Heighton, who read early versions of these stories and made invaluable suggestions for their improvement. The author is grateful to the editors of the publications where many of the pieces of this collection appeared first, in particular Susan Rendell, Janet Russell, Mark Jarman, David Carpenter, Dave Margoshes, Kim Jernigan, Rosalynn Tyo, Heidi Harms, Warren Cariou, Andris Taskans, Benjamin Wood, Mark Callanan and Michelle Butler Hallett. And for the contest alert, to Robert de Chazal, *mille mercis*.

"My Future in Insurance" was first published in *EarLit Shorts 3* (Rattling Books); "In the Wash" and "The Goddess Throws Down," in *The Fiddlehead*; "The Young in Their Country," in *Grain*; "Bluebird" (as "Bad Men Who Love Jesus"), "Mr. Greenaway Rights the Wrong" and "Speedwell," in *The New Quarterly*; "Oil & Sand" (as "Oil Sands") and "Hot Yoga," in *Prairie Fire*; "Doctor Mem" in PRISM *international*; and "High Hard" in *Riddle Fence*.